Praise for Walking The Wrong Way Home:

"Mandy Haynes has storytelling in her bones. If you've ever driven down a country road at night, seen a lone light in a distant farmhouse, and wondered what life is like for the people in that room—Mandy Haynes knows. Her stories give voice to the humor, sorrow, and sometimes even horror in the lives of people in the small towns and down the dirt roads of the South." Wayne Wood, author of Watching the Wheels: Cheap irony, righteous indignation and semi enlightened opinion

"It may be fiction but it's all true. Mandy writes razor-sharp, down-to-the bone southern tales about total strangers that you have known all your whole life. They jump off the page and grab you by the heart and they hang on long after the words have stopped. She knows us better than we know ourselves. This is the good stuff." Mike Henderson, singer/songwriter, musician, and all around badass

"Mandy Haynes has an amazing voice that reaches right into your gut. A talent like this is rare, and I look forward to seeing more from her soon." Nadia Bruce- Rawlings, Author of Scars

"Words and sentences are like music; the rhythms and the cadences wrap around you and pull you along. Mandy's work also like a heavy blanket on a good night's sleep. You don't want to end - the story or the sleep either one." Tommy Womack, singer-songwriter and author of Dust Bunnies, a memoir, Cheese Chronicles: The True Story of a Rock n Roll Band You've Never Heard Of, and the Lavender Boys and Elsie

"Mandy Haynes is a no-nonsense writer who cuts straight through to the core of what life is about with every character she creates. Each story is filled with an honest, raw, and beautiful dance that spotlights everyday people. Such a treat to read." Chuck Beard, freelance writer, editor, and author, owner of East Side Story

"Mandy Haynes doesn't write stories, she creates universes. From her mind comes people who inspire and infuriate and inform. They'll make you ache and smile and sigh, all at the same time." Peter Cooper, author of Johnny's Cash and Charlie's Pride: Lasting Legends and Untold Adventures in Country Music

WALKING THE WRONG WAY HOME

stories by

Mandy Haynes

*This book is dedicated to everyone who's
found themselves walking in the wrong direction.
It's never too late to find your way home.*

And to my son, Justin Groves. I love you.

You're still my favorite story.

"Hell, we cain't all be saints."

Penny, The Red Shoes

Table of Contents

Elma and Roy

Two Sides to Every Story

Elma - side one

*"...cain't so much as stick a candle on a
cold corn muffin and tell me happy
birthday."*

Today's my birthday. Don't seem to matter much, not
if I didn't even remember it my dang self. Once it was
pointed out to me, I had to stop and think to figure out
how old I was. Not that my age matters much neither.
Ain't like nobody's got reason to keep a record, but I'm
sure I would've thought about it after it'd come and
gone. Probably when I sat down to pay bills at the end
of the month. Lord knows, that can make you feel older
anyway.

Miss Rachel, though, she always remembers. She gave me a card with fifty dollars in it this morning. Had it sitting on the table propped up against the sugar bowl, her kitchen all nice and warm. The coffee already made. I knew by the smell coming from her oven she was baking those cinnamon rolls I love so much. That girl spoils me, treats me like I'm her favorite aunt instead of a paid employee.

I didn't know what to say when she told me to buy myself something special with the birthday gift. She usually gives me something that I wouldn't buy for myself, but this was the first time I'd ever gotten cash. I didn't tell her, but my first and only thought was to spend it on groceries. I could stock the pantry with the money before Roy found it and wasted it on who knows what. He wasn't a young man anymore, but you'd be surprised the women he could get with that quick smile and mouth full of lies. Especially if he had a fifty-dollar bill in his hand.

She's always been good to me, Miss Rachel. I been working for her for almost fifteen years. I do a little bit of everything around her house, but not a whole lot of anything. Not compared to other jobs I've had. She's always in the kitchen when I cook because she says she wants to learn everything I do. Says it would be a shame not to, since I don't follow recipes. I cook by sight and smell and I don't have to taste a roux to know if it's going to turn out.

At dinner time she does most of the cooking, but she acts like she cain't cook a lick. And she keeps her house so clean, there ain't much to do there neither. I tell her she needs to have a few young'uns to keep her busy, but she laughs and shakes her head. She says she's got other plans. Miss Rachel wants to run her own business, but she ain't sure just yet what it'll be. She said when she figures it out, she'll let me know. She's always going to meetings downtown and important parties at swanky places, so I spend most of my time sewing new dresses and suits for her. It's my favorite thing to do.

My mama taught me to sew before I could write. I ain't never followed a pattern. I make my own, so whatever I'm making comes out similar to the latest style, but different. I add little details that show off the material—not just the cut of the fabric.

Every type of material is different and should be treated as such. Miss Rachel swears I could make a fortune as a seamstress, but I cain't see the women around here giving up their shopping trips to Atlanta and their bragging rights on designer labels. She always pays me too much money for the dresses I make for her, in my opinion. But she says she'd pay twice as much if she bought them at a store. It almost feels like I'm stealing, because I enjoy it so much.

Plus, she went overboard when she turned one of her bedrooms into my very own space. I never had more than my kitchen table to work on when I sewed all my boys' clothes. Going into the sewing room she set up for me at her house is like walking into a toy store. Everything stays out, the bolts of fabric stacked up on a long shelf and pretty buttons and colorful spools of thread in jars like penny candy—lined up on shelves by the window. There's a long table set up just for cutting material and she bought a brand-new Singer machine just for me. When I'm in there sewin', I'm not working at all. It feels like play and I'd do it for nothing just to get to use that fancy machine. Plus, I'd never have a reason to sew all those smart looking suits and dresses or make anything with silk or fancy linen if it weren't for her.

Miss Rachel always keeps my sewing money and my house-keeping money separate, like the money I make sewing is special. I don't.

It all ends up going to the same bills.

I'd worked for her mother before she had a heart attack in '52, so I've known Miss Rachel since she was just a little, bitty thing. She was the prettiest baby I ever seen. Not like my own young'uns. Lord, they was ugly, all three of them. They come out mad and screaming and never stopped—being mad *or* screaming. I was hoping that they'd take after my side of the family, but they all turned out like their daddy. Not a nice thought between the four of them.

I bet none of them knows it's my birthday. I ain't never got so much as a card from one of them. Not even Roy.

I still make a fuss on their birthdays. I cook a big meal, with biscuits *and* cornbread, greens seasoned with fatback, black-eyed peas, pork chops, and fried chicken. All their favorites. Spend all day in the kitchen, bake them a cake with candles and everything. I guess I'm still holding on to the hope that they'll feel loved and maybe stop being so dang ornery and selfish. But that's foolishness, because even after all that fuss, not once have they even said so much as happy birthday to me. I used to tell myself stuff like that don't matter to men folk, but that's hard to believe when each one of them still shows up on their birthday, expecting a meal and a piece of birthday cake, even if I ain't seen them for months.

Quit thinking about that stuff, you old fool. They're your kids. You raised them, I tell myself. Don't do nothing but make me weary thinking about it anyway. Lots of things I wish I'd done different, but it's too late to fret over that now. My feet are tired, and my ankles are swollen something terrible. Miss Rachel told me to leave early today since it was my birthday, go do something for yourself she said, but I think she was just feeling sorry for me. She only told me to leave early once before—and, whew, what a day that was.

She'd taken me into town to help her pick out material and show me some patterns for a new dress. She liked my taste, she always said. I don't know about taste, but I do know what colors look good on her. Miss Rachel has the prettiest skin I've ever laid eyes on and the shiniest hair—and she don't even fuss with it like most of the women in her circle. She's a natural beauty inside and out. Sometimes she looks just like an angel. But not that day. Lord, no, not that day.

When we came back home from shopping, her husband was there. He wasn't alone, understand.

We walked in the kitchen and there they was, right on the countertop where I'd made breakfast. I remember thinking I was glad I'd wiped the counter good, because that lady's behind would sure be sticky. She was sitting—well, not exactly sitting—right where I'd whipped the honey that Mr. Garrett liked on his biscuits. In the kitchen of all places and in broad daylight.

Well, I ain't never been so embarrassed in my life. I

ain't never seen no white man's butt before. Lord, it could have glowed in the dark. It was a shock to me, and I am embarrassed to say I find myself thinking about it at the strangest times.

Miss Rachel came in right behind me, whatever she'd been saying forgotten. I turned to her just in time to see the pretty smile fall from her face. Then her face went blank. Scariest thing you ever seen, like Miss Rachel's insides had turned to ice. By the look in her eyes, it wasn't the first time she'd caught her husband in that kind of predicament. She asked me to leave. I didn't move fast enough or her, I reckon—what with the shock of what I'd just witnessed and all—because she took my arm and turned me towards the door.

"Miss Elma, why don't you take the rest of the day off?" she said, her voice as smooth as the silk we'd just bought in town. The look on her face was that of the devil hisself. I saw a hardness to her I'd never expected, and I was full of awe. But then I remembered that blinding white flesh behind me and I about plum yanked the doorknob off the door trying to get out of there. She didn't have to ask me twice. I wanted to be as far from that place as possible.

Someone said they saw her husband at the train station the next day with a black eye and his arm in a cast.

I would've never believed it if I hadn't seen Miss Rachel's face for myself. I never told nobody nothing about that day. It ain't none of their business no how. Nobody seemed to care when it was me that was hurt. No sir, they minded their own just fine. I figured Mr. Garrett was a grown man, he could take care of hisself.

I guess they worked things out, because he's back now. But you can believe I'm always careful to make noise before I enter a room when he's home.

That first day I left early was the day I found out who was leaving money under my rocking chair. The first time I didn't know what to do. I kept it hidden in the flour bin until a second envelope showed up with a letter stuffed inside.

The letter said to please take the money and don't ask questions. It was addressed to me. Well, I did, and I didn't ask. Times were hard and Roy wasn't much for counting on. He'd spend his money on whatever he wanted, never thinking about me or the boys. When they was little I used to wonder how we was ever gonna make it. It's funny how you just do, ain't it?

He was something else, that husband of mine. There was a time I thought he loved me. But then I realized he just wanted a place to sleep when his girlfriends' husbands came home. Someone to cook his meals when he was hungry, do his laundry when it was dirty, and keep his house in order.

Speaking of, that was who was leaving the money. Well, a young girl he wished was his girlfriend anyway, but this girl was smarter than the others. Ernetta was one of the girls that worked at the bait shop. She was a pretty little thing, couldn't have been much older than my middle son. She liked to have died when I walked up on her.

Ernetta didn't speak for a few minutes, then she started in. "I ain't lying with your husband, ma'am. He won't leave me alone. I don't ask for nothing, and I ain't giving him nothing, but he still won't stop hanging around."

I could tell by the way she pulled on the hem of her shirt she was scared, the poor child. I shrugged my shoulders at what she was saying, too tired to say anything back. Still trying to get the picture of Mr. Garrett's backside out of my mind.

She started crying. "He tries to buy me stuff and he acts like he and his boys are made of money, but I know different. I know your son, Leroy. I know he ain't barely got a pot to piss in. I reckon Roy wouldn't neither, if it wasn't for you." Ernetta stopped to wipe her eyes on the back of one hand. "I don't want his money. He tips me big sometimes for selling him cigarettes or beer, and when he does, I bring it here. I hope you ain't mad. I don't mean to hurt your pride."

"Listen to me, child, don't you worry your pretty little head over none of it. I appreciate your kindness, but if he tips you again, you keep the money. You deserve it for having to put up with his nonsense. I consider myself lucky, being that he don't want nothing from me no more."

That made her laugh, just a little hiccup of a laugh, but still, it was better than tears. I knew her mama died when she was still in diapers and this girl ain't had an easy life herself. Her daddy was a good man, but he was left with a house full of young'uns when his wife died and never remarried. Poor Ernetta had to grow up fast. She reminded me of a little bird, pecking and scratching to survive.

Every once in a while, I'll still get an envelope from her.

I'd hoped that she'd get out of this town. There ain't a whole lot for girls like her around here, except men like Roy.

I remember once a long time ago when Roy and I'd only been married a few years. One morning Roy woke up and started crying. Looked right at me, sobbing like a baby, right there in our bed.

I asked him what was wrong, and he said he'd dreamt that he was married to a beautiful, young girl with long hair and pretty teeth. She had bright eyes and soft skin. He was crying because he realized that it was just a dream. Had the nerve to tell me that and not feel the least bit ashamed.

I didn't know what to say, so I didn't say nothing. I laid there and listened to him cry and feel sorry for hisself.

I think that was when I stopped feeling anything for him. Wasn't long after that I stopped feeling much of anything at all. There was a time when I was a pretty, young girl myself. I had soft hands before I had to keep them in lye soap all day. I used to have pretty, smooth skin before I got pregnant with his babies.

My eyes. I used to have the prettiest eyes in town. I don't mean to sound full of myself, but everyone used to stop my mama to tell her so. Mama said she used to love to make me laugh, because of the way my eyes lit up. I used to laugh all the time, but that was before I got a tooth knocked loose and this scar across my right eyebrow.

That was thanks to Roy. He had a temper and didn't mind using it. After that night, when he put that gash across my eye, worried that he'd blinded me, he never hit me in the face again. It didn't really matter to me, a bruise is a bruise, no matter where it is.

Lord have mercy, woman, what are you trying to do to yourself? I asked myself. I shook my head and tried to change the path that my mind was taking. All that is water under the bridge. *Water under a bridge you yourself burnt up years ago, when you decided to stay.*

I thought of my sister. I tried not to think about her too much, because it makes me so lonesome it almost swallows me up. Eliza, Elizabeth she liked to be called now, had moved to Philadelphia a long time ago. She's a lawyer, that baby sister of mine. She was always smart and headstrong—even as a child she stood her ground and fought for what she wanted. I used to have to threaten her with a switch some days when she refused to do her chores, but more often than not, I'd do her load so she could read her schoolbooks and study. Mama used to say I spoiled her, but truth be told I'd admired her spirit and didn't want to tame it. When Eliza moved away I was as proud of her as if she'd been my own child. No holding that girl down, no, sir. The last time she was here, she begged me to come back with her, but there was just no way I could up and move to Philadelphia. I had three young boys to raise. But they're all grown now. Grown and moved on. I haven't seen her in years, but I knew she was still in the same place, because she sent me a letter every couple of months. The last one'd come just a few days before and it ended the same as the others. My baby sister telling me to come live with her, that she had a room with a view of her rose garden set up just for me.

I'd read each letter standing at my kitchen sink, looking out into the backyard at my little vegetable garden. What we didn't eat during the summer, I'd can or freeze to eat through the winter. Even the marigolds I planted served a purpose, they were there to keep the pests away from the vegetables. I couldn't imagine having the time to work in a garden just to fill a vase with pretty smelling flowers.

Lordy, I would love to see her, but she won't come down this way no more, not after our mama and daddy passed on. Eliza says she misses me, and I believe she does, but she hates Roy more than she loves me and she don't mind telling him neither. She says she can't stand to see the look in my eyes. I don't know what it is she's talking about exactly. I never look in a mirror no more, so I don't know what look I got in my eyes.

I don't know what's wrong with me today, but now I'm missing my sister something fierce. I've been in a foul mood ever since I remembered it was my birthday.

I am sixty-three years old today.

I ain't never done nothing for myself. Not in sixty-three years. I ain't never been nowhere, except this little town. I spent my whole life taking care of four men who couldn't care less about me, who cain't so much as stick a candle in a cold corn muffin and tell me happy birthday.

My mama died when she was sixty-two.

I took a deep breath and realized I was just walking blind, so lost in my thoughts. I'd meant to go home, but I was walking the wrong way. I was going towards town, so I figured I'd just keep on going and spend my birthday money on groceries. Ain't nothing else to spend it on that wouldn't be a waste. But the thought of doing that made me hurt deep down and all over. I was tired of feeling this way. I was scared of spending the rest of my life without actually living a minute of it.

I looked up and found myself outside the bus station. Miss Rachel's voice ringing in my ears, telling me to do something special for myself. Less than an hour ago, I'd had no idea what that would be. Next thing I knew, I was walking through the door and up to the ticket booth, holding the money from Miss Rachel in my hand.

I asked for a one-way ticket to Philadelphia.

A lady walked by wearing rose scented perfume and I laughed out loud for the first time in ages, not caring how I looked to her or the man behind the counter. The smell of roses had to be a sign I was heading in the right direction. Let them all think I was crazy, maybe I was, but I didn't think so.

I felt my heart beating inside my ribcage—a feeling I'd long forgotten.

It was the feeling of being alive.

Roy - side two

"It ain't easy being me. See my last name, it's Freeman—free man—it ain't my fault, it's a curse."

That ol' woman has done finally lost her mind. Elma left this morning without fixing me my breakfast. She must've been real quiet too, because I didn't hear her leave for work. 'Course I was sleeping like a bear, seeing as I didn't come in until around two o'clock this morning. I figured she would be in a mood, it being her birthday, so I thought I'd save myself the misery and came in a little later than usual.

Ain't no woman past twenty-one happy 'bout getting older, that's a fact, and I didn't see no sense in letting her bring me down. I'd had a good day yesterday—I won forty dollars at the track and found another ten dollars on my way in, I didn't need no grumbling from Elma to wreck my good mood.

Yep, yesterday was a good day indeed. I found the ten-dollar bill in an envelope on the front porch.

I figured it must've fell out of the ol' woman's pocket as she was coming in, probably a little extra from her boss for polishing the silver or some nonsense like that. Good thing it'd gotten caught under the runner of the rocking chair—it'd been a shame if neither one of us could spend it.

I check the oven for my leftover dinner from the night before. Elma knows to leave me a plate, I taught her that early on. I might not feel like eating when it's ready, but it better be ready when I feel like eating.

"Well, goddamn." The oven is as empty as the stovetop was bare.

I stop and think for a second. Had she been sick? She hadn't missed work, but that don't mean nothing. She would have to be on her death bed before she missed a day at Miss Rachel's house. She gets a steady check from her job as Miss Rachel's slave, but I wouldn't work for no white people, no, sir, cleaning their house, taking care of their property. Not me. Not Roy Freeman Jr., no, sir.

Elma, the ol' fool, seems to like it, not only like it, she's actually proud of her job. She thinks of them rich white folks as friends, some kinda family. Which I told her real quick was a bunch of horse shit. She ain't nothing but the help. But it beats working at the cotton mill, I guess. Not that I'd ever worked in no mill, but I've heard stories.

"What's gotten into that ol' fool?" I ask. I'm alone but I talk out loud just the same. "Turns sixty-seven and loses what little sense she ever had."

I do this a lot, talk to myself. Sometimes I'm the only one who understands me. Nobody knows how hard it is to be Roy Freeman Jr. See my last name, it's Freeman—free man—it ain't my fault, it's a curse. I ain't supposed to be tied down, I need to be able to spread my wings when the urge hits me. And sometimes I just need to talk to someone who's got some sense. Hard to find in this pissant town.

My stomach is growling so loud I can hardly hear myself talk. I need to get some food in me so I can drink some whiskey. I look back in the icebox, but it appears to me that there ain't nothing in there that doesn't need to be cooked first. I ain't exactly sure. Like I said before, I always have my meals waiting for me. I ain't never had to make no food.

There's buttermilk, but what good's buttermilk if there ain't no cornbread to go with it? I check the pantry. A bag of beans as hard as rocks, rice, flour, some cornmeal, raisins, oats, and some other stuff, but I get tired of trying to figure out what it all is. I ain't much of a reader.

I grab a handful of oats and put it in a bowl. Then a

handful of raisins, add them to the oats and pour buttermilk on top. It looks pretty good but tastes worse than turkey shit. I spit it out so quick that half of it hits the floor in front of the sink. How'd Elma make them eatable? Well, who knows and who cares—I ain't wasting my patience on it because I got fifty dollars in my pocket and a sunny day ahead of me.

I leave my mess right where it is and decide to go on down to Sadie's for breakfast. It's only ten o'clock, so there'll still be some old farts there drinking coffee. Hell, the good gossip ain't even had time to make the second round yet.

Even though I'm nearly starved, it's a beautiful day to be walking on Main Street. I have some money in my pocket, about to get a good meal cooked by a nice-looking young gal. I have a flask of some of the best 'shine ever made in my hip pocket and I'm pretty sure I'm gonna have a good supper waiting on me tonight— even if I don't eat it until tomorrow. I bet that ol' woman cooks a feast to make up for not cooking me my breakfast this morning and not making me a dinner plate the night before.

You know, I bet she had to go into work early and didn't want to wake me by making a racket in the kitchen. Surely that's it. She's never not cooked my breakfast, not once in all the years we've been married.

Maybe one of our boys stopped by for dinner last night. That would explain why I didn't have a dinner plate, because those boys can put away some food. If that's the case, I'm glad I wasn't there, seeing as how I'm running low on liquor and I owe Jeremiah thirty dollars. It'll pay off for me in the end. She'll make me a feast and I didn't have to share my stash. And if I'm real lucky, Jeremiah would've asked his mama for the money I borrowed. Elma cain't never say no to her youngest son, and I won't have to let go of my hard earned cash.

She'll get home from work, see the remains of the pitiful meal I had to suffer through, and probably even bake me a buttermilk pie—which she should, because she knows I wake up hungry.

Elma bakes the best pies in all of Tennessee. That and her pretty eyes were what made me ask her to marry me.

Well, that and the fact that man in Birmingham was chasing after me to marry his daughter. I wasn't about to have no shotgun wedding. What a mistake that would've been—that old man would've tried to make me a sharecropper like him.

And that girl had two mean older brothers. Elma didn't have no family, 'cept for a little sister and a mama that was as old as Methuselah, so it was an easy choice to make.

But Elma's eyes ain't so pretty no more. She looks like an ol' workhorse. Her hands feel like leather and her face has deep wrinkles in it. Her hair is still long, like I like it, but it's full of white streaks. Ain't as nice as it used to be, and she don't never take it down like she used to. Plus, Elma got kinda thick after our third son was born and never got her shape back. Don't get me wrong, ain't nothing wrong with a little meat on the bone, but her back looks rounded and her feet look heavy, like she's toting the weight of the world on her shoulders.

She quit carrying herself like those young girls at the bait shop way before she should've. She always looks tired and I cain't figure out why. Working for Miss Rachel couldn't be that hard. Hell, she only has to walk a mile to get to work each day. Well, two if you add coming back home, but still, I walk that far to the track and back just about every day. No big deal. And our kids practically raised themselves. Seemed like I just started noticing them and they was off to school. The next thing I knew, they was working their own jobs and moving on. They couldn't have been that much trouble. At least they was boys.

There's a good crowd at Sadie's which can be a blessing or a curse. I find a seat at a booth out of the way and sit down. I was hoping to get that good-looking new girl to wait on me, but Viola sees me first. Shit.

"Hey, Roy." She pours my coffee and asks me what I want. The way she runs her tongue over her top lip lets me know she ain't talking about biscuits and gravy.

"Just give me my usual, Viola, and try not to make a damn fool out of yourself," I say, deciding to nip any nonsense she might throw at me in the bud. It's a gamble, but it works. She puts her tongue back in her mouth and leaves me be.

Somehow, Viola got it in her head that she's my girlfriend.

Just because I took her dancing and bought her a few drinks. Just because I stayed over one night. Just because she let me borrow twenty dollars.

Ern sees me and waves me over to the empty stool beside him at the counter. He used to be sweet on Elma, but that was years ago. It ain't no secret that I don't really care for Ern, but on the other hand—if I sat there at the counter, Viola won't be waiting on me. I get up so quick I almost spill my coffee.

"Mornin', old man." He pats me on the back. I cain't help but notice he looks unusually happy this morning.

"Who you calling old man, old man?" He had to have at least five years on me.

"You looking kinda sour this morning. Elma finally pack up and leave you?" He must think he's real funny.

The way he laughs into his coffee cup makes me want to ram it down his throat.

"Where would an old battle-ax like Elma go, Ern? Hell, she ain't about to set off on her own, and there ain't no man in his right mind that'd want her. Shit, I don't even want her, and I'm married to her," I say with a grin, determined not to let him see my anger.

That gets everybody sitting at the counter laughing. That's what I love about this place—a man can be a man here. The only women around are the ones waiting on you and making sure your coffee cup is full. They never let your coffee get cold, and if you're lucky, you can catch a glimpse of that soft line squished together down the middle of their chests—everybody knows Sadie's has the best uniforms for us boob men.

My food comes and I eat it right quick. The fellas are quiet, which is unusual—there ain't any good gossip, I guess. Everybody's silent except for an occasional chuckle here and there. I must've missed the joke, or maybe they're laughing at Viola pouting over at the other end of the counter. If that's the case, I don't want to be in on that. I ain't pushing my luck with her no further than I already have. She has a bad temper, and she outweighs me by twenty pounds at least. I leave as soon as I finish the last bite of my ham biscuit.

I have things to do and money burning a hole in my pocket. As I'm leaving, I see Miss Rachel's car pull up to the curb. For one second she looks like she's gonna say something to me, but I act like I don't see her. I cain't stand no uppity woman.

She would have Elma move in with her just for spite and leave me on my own if she could. Anyway, I walk on past like she ain't there. I could swear I hear her laugh as I walk by.

Doggone, people sure are acting strange today.

I make it on down to the track, but luck ain't on my side and I lose twenty dollars. Oh well, I ain't ever unlucky for long.

I'm getting tired, so I go on back home. Thinking I'll take a nap before time for Elma to get in. If I plan it right, I can get home, take a nap, and then get back out before she comes in to start my supper. That way she'll think I been out working and won't ask me no questions. Not that she ever does, but I still don't want to give her the wrong impression. I am a busy man after all,

On the way up the walk I take a good look at our house. It looks different to me, but I ain't sure why. The porch is swept clean like always, the rockers are sitting there side by side under the window, which should be inviting, but that window looks like an eye staring me down.

I go on through the door and lay right there on the couch. For some reason I don't want to walk through the house to lie on the bed, the hallway to our bedroom looks longer than it really is and full of shadows. The air feels heavy and musty—I was giving myself the willies.

I haven't gotten my imagination worked up like this since I was a boy. When I was a young'un, I used to scare myself so bad that most times I wouldn't make it to the outhouse. I'd just let it rip right there off the back porch. If I was lucky, I could take care of business without my mama knowing. Whowee, she'd throw a fit if she caught me peeing on her flowerbed, but it was worth the risk not to have to walk out in the dark once I got those scary thoughts swirling around in my head.

My mama used to say it was a guilty conscious that caused me to feel that way. Guilty? Hell, like Pappy always said, you ain't guilty if you ain't caught.

Whatever it is, guilty conscious or real haints running around the house, I get myself spooked and start feeling mighty lonesome. I sit up, too jittery now to keep my eyes closed. I refill my flask from the jar I keep hidden under the couch, and head on out to see what's going on at the bait shop.

Turns out nothing much is going on. The new girl ain't

much of a talker no matter how hard I try or how much I tip her. But I seen her grinning at Towry once and hell, if she can give that old ugly sumbitch a grin then I know I still got a chance. But, I ain't used to working so hard to get a grin outta them gals. And today I just don't have it in me to try, so I take a stroll to the river instead. I sip on my flask and sit on one of the big rocks overlooking the water to watch them ol' soft shell turtles basking in the sun.

When I was a boy, we'd shoot them turtles with our slingshots and my mama would make a pot of soup with 'em. They's awful stringy, but she could make 'em taste real good. It's been a long time since I got one—don't know if I'd still be able to if I tried.

I hate to admit it, but I ain't a young man anymore.

My hands ain't as steady as they used to be.

Thinking about turtle soup makes me think about my mama. Thinking about my mama makes me think about my pappy. Thinking about my pappy always put me in a sad state. So I sit there for a while, feeling sorry for myself and getting good and drunk. I'm not sure what time or exactly how I made it home, but I wake up on the front porch with the sun in my eyes.

I ain't never woke up on the front porch. Elma's never left me out there before.

That ol' woman must be sulking because I didn't get

her no birthday present. She ain't never carried on like this in all the years we've been married.

Well, she can sulk all she wants. I think the fresh air did me some good. Come to think of it, a change of scenery will do me even better. I think I might take off down the road a piece, let her miss me for a while. Make her see how foolish she's bein'. I got a lady friend in Lexington I ain't seen in a while I'm sure will be glad to see me. Always is, and she knows how to treat a man.

I don't know how to explain it, but it's all I can do to make myself go into that house. Looking at the door is giving me the shivers. It seems so *empty*.

I hurry in just long enough to change my clothes and wash my face. I grab my toothbrush and stick it in the bib pocket of my overalls. I go right back out the way I came in, never walking into the kitchen to see what Elma might have left for me on the stove.

"Too little, too late," I say out loud to cut through the silence as I hurry down the steps. Two can play this game, you ol' hardheaded nag.

I'm in luck. I haven't made it no more than a mile down the road when someone pulls up beside me in a pickup.

"You headed to Philadelphia?" Ern asks with a grin.

Philadelphia? What an idgit. Why in the hell would I be going to Philadelphia?

"Nope, fool, I'm headed over to Lexington for a day or two. Got me a little business to take care of." I try not to look at him because his grin is getting on my last nerve.

"Lexington? Well, it's your lucky day. That's where I'm headed. Hop in and I'll give you a ride."

I think about it for a minute or two, but in the end, my tired, old feet beat out my pride. As much as I hate that old fart, I cain't pass up his offer.

It really must be my lucky day because Ern ain't in a talking mood. He's in a laughing, singing, looking like a fool mood instead, but at least he ain't trying to get in my business. My curiosity almost gets the best of me and I nearly ask him why he's in such good spirits, but I'm able to stop myself before that happens. I don't want to know why he's so happy. Matter of fact, it chaps my ass just a little bit.

Just when I think I cain't take it no more, we pull into town. I open my door at the first stop sign we come to.

"Will you be wanting a ride back?" he asks me.

"No, it might take me a while to get caught up on my business here." I flash him my best shit-eating grin and give him a wink. That usually gives me some satisfaction, but I'll be damned if that ol' bastard didn't laugh in my face as he pulls away.

I walk on down the road a bit until I come to an old

run-down beer joint. My favorite kind. I go in and order a cold one and two pickled eggs. I reach in my pocket and pull out my little wad of cash, intending on paying with the ten-dollar bill I found on the porch, but I just cain't bring myself to let it go. I hand the bartender my twenty instead. I drink my beer and check out the bar for prospects. There ain't no women around, so I go to the back and use a payphone to call my lady friend.

Told you it was my lucky day. She ain't home, but her younger sister is. Said she remembers me, and she would love to meet me for a beer. If my memory serves me correctly, she's quite a looker. Dang knockout a couple of years ago. Big, hazel eyes and pretty, dark skin. I go back to the bar to wait on her.

Well, I must've had the wrong little sister in mind, because the girl that walks up to me thirty minutes later ain't nowhere near sweet, don't have pretty or dark skin, and her eyes are too small in her flat round face. Lordy, she is a sight. But beggars cain't be choosers. Plus, I won't be here more than a day or two, and sometimes the ugly girls turn out to be the most fun anyways.

Well, it would've been okay except for the carload of kids waiting on us when we left an hour later. That wouldn't have been so bad either if the daddy of two of those kids wasn't sitting in his car behind them waiting on their mama.

Lordy, I was scared for a second, I'll admit—I'm a lover, not a fighter—but then I realize he just wants some money from her. I cain't help but notice the nice stack of bills she has in her purse.

Things are looking up. Maybe she'll loan me a little cash and her sister can pay her back when she comes home.

I ask her about a loan, and she says she'll do even better than that—she'll pay double what I asked for to watch her kids for a couple of hours. I ain't sure how it happened …

I think she put some kind of voodoo on me. A couple of hours turned into damn near a week and I babysat those snot-nosed kids while she was out doing God knows what all. I was just glad to get out of there when I did, stealing a change of clothes I found left by some other poor fool and two dollars from one of the heathens' piggybanks for my effort. I don't know how I made it out alive—those kids were like wild animals. Every time I tried to sneak out, one of 'em would cling to my leg while another one would climb on my back. I threatened to skin them alive, but the meanest one threatened to call the law. I didn't need no more trouble with the police in Lexington, so we came to a truce. At least the oldest girl knew how to cook a decent pan of biscuits, or we'd all starved to death.

I was thinking about heading back home, but I ran

into an old friend of mine. Or rather, Jackson about ran me over as I was crossing Main St. He invited me to come back to his place, so I took him up on the offer. Me and Jackson used to run a little moonshine together and had us a pretty good poker scam back when we was younger.

I was hoping to relive a little of our past, but ol' Jackson had changed. He'd found religion and married a young girl from his church. Became a Deacon.

Damnedest thing you ever saw.

Jackson and his wife live in a big fine house, complete with a damn white picket fence, over on Rosewood. She's a pretty thing with nice soft curves, I'll give him that, but she cain't cook nowhere near as good as Elma. And she's bossy. I finally get it sorted out that Jackson ain't running another scam. He's actually proud of his sass talking, bible thumping, wife and he ain't interested in any kind of fun no more.

I decide to head back home. Surely Elma is through sulking by now.

I make it halfway home, wishing I could catch a ride, when who should I see coming up the road in her brand-new Cadillac but Miss Rachel. She pulls over to ask if I want a ride.

Well, I let my aching bones win over my pride once again. I sink down in the soft leather seat and regret it almost at once.

"So, how are you getting along?" she asks, sounding concerned, and it's a little too personal for my liking.

"Mighty fine." I wink at her to show her just how fine I am.

Miss Rachel looks shocked, which is good. That's what I was hoping for, but then she starts in about Elma. Elma this and Elma that, on and on she clucks like an old hen until I finally roll down the window and let the wind drown her out.

I don't need her to tell me anything about my own wife. She's mine, I know her better than anybody else. Either Miss Rachel gets the point, or she just gets tired of her hair flying in her mouth, but either way she finally shuts up.

She pulls up to the curb outside of Sadie's and I get out without a word. But then she says something that don't make no sense.

She says, "Roy, I'm glad you're doing fine, because I was almost beginning to feel sorry for you." I turn to look at her, and she shakes her head. "To think, I was even feeling a little guilty."

"Guilty for what?" I start to ask, but she pulls away without giving me the chance. I'm glad I'm standing outside of the diner, because all of a sudden I'm hungry as a horse. Viola's at the counter laughing so hard she's about in tears.

Ern's telling something that has everybody listening. For some reason I don't like the looks on their faces when I walk in the door, but I walk on up to the counter and order coffee anyways.

"Well, I reckon you're 'bout starved this morning. You want some grits and eggs to go with your usual ham biscuit?" Viola asks, looking like some old cat that's swallowed a bird.

"Did I ask for grits and eggs?" I answer back, start to tell a lie about the feast Elma made for me that mornin', but my stomach growls so loud right then it gives me away.

"Someone's in a mood this morning," she says, that sly grin still on her face as she turns to get my coffee.

"Seems like you'd be in a good mood, what with the news about Elma and all," Ern says as he turns all the way around to face me. For some reason I cain't look him in the eye. I cain't do nothing but sit there, looking at the counter.

"Lord knows if I was married to such a smart woman, I'd be a happy man."

I feel like all the air's being sucked right out of me.

"I know my Ernetta is as smart as she is pretty. You know my baby girl, don't you, Roy? You act a fool over her at the bait shop. Well, she's awful excited. Sounds like Elma put in a good word for her with Miss Rachel. Yes, sir. She called me last night to tell me all about it. She thinks

42

they all gonna make a fortune. What, with Miss Rachel's money and connections, and Elma's common sense and sewing skills, my girl thinks they are on to something big. Thinks they might just give those New York designers a run for their money. Lordy be." He stops to take a sip of coffee, "'Course, my baby girl will just be a salesgirl once they get opened up, not a fancy designer like Elma, but she says Elma wants to teach her everything she knows. Miss Rachel wants everyone to have a share in the business and everyone knows Miss Rachel's word is as good as gold."

I turn around to look at him and see that everyone at the counter is staring at me.

"You think you'll be movin' out to Philadelphia any time soon?" George asks with the same shit-eating grin I'd used on Ern a few of days ago.

I get up and walk out. Just leave my coffee on the counter and go out the door, feeling the weight of everybody's eyes on me. It's so quiet at the counter the bell over the door sounds ten times louder than normal. I fight the urge to yank it down and throw it in Ern's face. If I hadn't gotten so tired all of a sudden, I would've. I walk home without taking my eyes off my feet.

Philadelphia?

I'd been gone about a week and a half. Elma couldn't have gotten up the nerve to go to Philadelphia. Shit, she ain't never been nowhere. She wouldn't just up and go to *Philadelphia*. That old bat wouldn't leave me. I was her husband. I was the only family she had left. Well, except for our sons. And her sister. *Who lives in Philadelphia.* My stomach cramps something fierce.

I reach for my flask forgetting it's empty.

All this is a bunch of Ern's horse shit trying to mess with my mind. Elma some kinda fancy designer? She ain't nothing but a housekeeper. There will be a pie in the oven waiting for me when I get home and a pot of beans on the stove. She'll have made me a skillet of cornbread to make up for treating me so terrible.

My hands are shaking so bad I shove them in my pockets so I won't have to see them.

I look up at the house, the same house Elma and I've been living in for the last forty years. Why would she leave?

I'm hit with a lonesome so heavy I cain't hardly keep from falling to my knees.

"Elma!" I look around to make sure no one's listening. I hadn't meant to call her name out loud.

I walk into the kitchen and stop there in the doorway; I feel like I've been kicked in the gut by a mule.

There in the sink, and on the floor in front of the cabinet, is the mess I'd made almost two weeks ago. There's the bowl of uncooked oatmeal I'd tried to eat for breakfast.

Everything sitting right where I left it— as scary as any haint I've ever imagined.

"Elma!"

I walk into our bedroom and look in the closet. Her dresses, lifeless and faded, are still hanging on the hangers. I check the nightstand. Her bible is there. The soft worn leather of the cover, staring at me, mocking me. Judging me.

She'd left without taking a single thing. "Elma!" I yell, but I knew she wouldn't answer.

There ain't no one in this house but me.

I sit on my side of the bed and cry—hot tears that seem to burn my face. Cry for everything I'd ever lost. My mama, my pappy, my youth. I cry until I think I might die. I let them ol' haints dance all around me, let my imagination get the best of me.

I don't know if I'm ever gonna stop these tears once they start. What am I gonna do? Who's gonna take care of me now?

How am I supposed to make it without Elma? The Elma I'd known for damn near fifty years. The Elma that took care of me and always chased those haints away—not even knowing she was doing it. The Elma that used to sing in our kitchen when she made my biscuits.

The Elma that always bakes me a cake on my

birthday. The Elma that knew her place.

That Elma is gone. I am sure of that more than I've ever been sure of anything in my life, and the thought scares me to death.

That Elma, *my* Elma, is gone for good.

She Said

*"I thought she was allergic to dogs.
She said he's not a dog, he's a poodle."*

The new and obnoxious French Provincial style clock that hangs over my desk says it's five o'clock. I stand, careful not to hit my head on the tacky scrollwork and push my chair under the desk. As I lift my coat from the hook in the corner I immediately miss my old cardigan sweater. The new coat is too stiff, too tight through the shoulders and the material is scratchy—plus it smells funny. Come to think of it, all my new clothes smell funny. The entire new wardrobe. She said I needed to change the way I dress if I want to get anywhere in this company.

I liked my comfortable sweater. She said it made me

look like Mr. Rogers. I'd thought that was a compliment, but she said Mr. Rogers had zero sex appeal and was a wuss.

I used to love coming to work, but since my title changed, I dread it. I mean, I like my co-workers—or I liked them when they *were* my co-workers. Now they're technically my employees.

The new position is stressful. Things have really changed since they made me vice president, but she said I would be crazy to pass up the promotion.

I hate being called boss. She said it's sexy. Wednesdays used to be my favorite day of the week. In the old days I'd go bowling after work, but now I go straight home. She said if I wanted my employees to respect me, I shouldn't spend so much time with them outside the office. She said I needed to distance myself from them so they would take me more seriously.

On my way out, I see that Sally, the receptionist, has turned off her computer and is searching through her purse for her keys. I notice her look up, but I avert my eyes and walk past the front desk without stopping. Just a few months ago I would've waited until she had her things together, then walked her to her car. This isn't the safest neighborhood, you know. But I'd made the mistake of answering my cell phone one afternoon while I was standing at the desk waiting for Sally.

She wanted to know why I hadn't left yet. She told me I would get rumors started around the office, and people were probably already talking about the way I hung around Sally's desk. She said it didn't look right, the way we always left together, and made me promise to stop.

I walk to my old clunker on the far side of the parking lot. It's got close to two hundred thousand miles on it, and since my promotion, a few new dents and suspicious scratches. Three months ago, I started car shopping. I had my eye on one of those new four door pickups, but she said it would be a waste of money to buy *two* new vehicles. She said we didn't need a truck.

I thought she'd think a truck was sexy, but she said trucks were stupid.

The light turns red at the intersection and I notice a sign for a new pizza place on the corner. I love pizza. I used to have one delivered every Sunday afternoon and eat it while I watched movies on the Classic Movie Channel. She said she hated pizza.

I used to love watching old black-and-white movies.

She said they gave her migraines.

I used to listen to the local talk station when I was in my car. My favorite show was this guy who would play old blues and jazz tunes and have people call in to guess the artist. I haven't listened to it in so long, I don't even know if I could find the station. She said talk radio made her anxious.

I used to love to listen to the blues. She said they were depressing.

My car seems to be on autopilot as it heads towards the new house. I used to live on the other side of town, in a little neighborhood off Walnut Street. It was a nice place. Cozy, with a small garden in the back and a place for my dog, Larry, to run.

But she said the neighborhood was being overrun with *suspicious characters*. She said she didn't feel comfortable there alone when I was at work.

Raul and Alejandra were the best neighbors ever. The three of us would get together with Jamel and Ameenha who lived across the street and work in the community garden we'd planted at the end of the cul-de-sac. On Sundays we'd have a potluck with the vegetables we raised and share a bottle of home-brewed beer or two. She said they scared her, and she didn't like beer.

The new house is twice the size of the other one. A two story McMansion with a huge porch but sits on a lot that's half the size of the old house. The yard is the size of a postage stamp, with no room for a big dog to run around. But I had to find a new home for Larry anyway. She said she was allergic to dogs. I still can't believe I let him go; he was my best friend.

I'm not ashamed to say I cried when his new family picked him up and drove away. She said I had a weird attachment to my dog.

I pull into my driveway and park in front of the garage door out of habit. She said there wasn't enough room for my old car and her Expedition in the garage.

I walk to the mailbox and notice my neighbor, Mike, in his front yard and wave before I can stop myself. He doesn't wave back. He's an arrogant asshole. She said he was a wonderful man.

I said he was a conceited steroid junkie. She said I should go to the gym more often.

I said I would go to the gym with her. She said she needed her *alone time*.

One afternoon through his big picture window I saw him slide his hand up Martina's skirt as she was dusting the light fixture in his kitchen. Martina kicked at his head, almost falling off the ladder in the process. I was watching the whole thing from our back deck as I was starting the grill. I like charcoal, but she said gas was cleaner.

Anyway, I told her what the jerk had done and asked what we should do. She said there was no way he would stoop so low as to hit on the *hired help*.

I told her Martina seemed like a nice kid. She said

Martina wasn't from this country and probably didn't speak English. She said Martina liked the attention or she wouldn't wear short skirts. She said you can't trust anybody who doesn't speak English.

Just as I am going through the front door, Mike's little designer dog runs over and hikes his leg on my roses. He's a nippy thing, not friendly like good old Larry, probably pissed off because Mike's wife dresses him up in ridiculous outfits and carries him around in her purse. I feel for him, but I wish he'd stay out of our yard. If he's not pissing on my roses, he's taking a shit by my mailbox or trying to bite my ankle. I told her if she wouldn't call him over and make such a fuss over him, he'd stay in his own yard. I told her I thought she was allergic to dogs. She said he's not a *dog*, he's a *poodle*.

I take off my jacket as soon as the front door closes, putting it and the new expensive wing tips in the hall closet. I used to keep my clothes in the bedroom closet, but she said she needed more room for her shoes.

Suddenly it hit me, a switch flips as I stand there, alone in my house.

I walk into the kitchen, pick up the phone, and order a pizza. I take off my tie and stuff it in the garbage disposal, realizing that's a mistake as soon as I turn it on. I laugh out loud as the contraption shakes hard enough to knock the soap dish into the sink before the motor grinds to a stop. I haven't laughed in weeks. Months maybe. To hell with it, I laugh again, and I like the way it feels. I never wanted the damn disposal anyway. I think I'll build a compost bin and start another garden. Invite my old neighbors over for a beer.

I turn on the radio that sits on the counter and find my show just in time to catch the last half of a Meade Lux Lewis number. I can't help but grin at the irony.

Singing with Lewis to Low Down Dog, I go to the basement, get my bowling ball and put it by the front door. I stop on my way through the den to turn on the TV and put it on the Classic Movie Channel.

Back in the kitchen I find the Christmas card from the smiling family who adopted Larry. He looks happy with his new owners, but I miss that sweet old hound. Of all the dumb things I've done in the last year, being manipulated by a set of double D's and a blinding smile—neither of which were real—letting go of Larry was the dumbest. Being lonely can make a person do some crazy shit, but I realize I wasn't lonely when I had Larry by my side. I was blindsided by pheromones.

I'll call them tomorrow and offer to dog sit whenever they need it—or what the hell, I'll ask for joint custody. Maybe they'll share him on the weekends or something.

Feeling better than I have in months, I take the paper to the table and look for a good deal on a new truck while I wait on the pizza delivery guy.

She said she was the best thing that ever happened to me.

She said the best day in my life was when she said *I do*.

She said I would be lonely and sorry if she left.

She lied.

The Red Shoes

"Hell, we cain't all be saints."

When Charlene asked if I'd like to read something to the group in place of our typical game of Bingo on Thursday, I jumped at the chance. Anything was better than having to listen to poor Margo cry out *"B3? B3?"* twice in the same week. Bless her heart, she cain't hear worth a damn and her eyesight's about shot, which gives Bingo a whole new twist. And not in a good way. The natives are restless, Charlene told me, and one night of Bingo a week is plenty. And since she was the person in charge of activities here at Azalea Court, she had the final say. Charlene wasn't heartless, Margo could still get dolled up like Vanna White and flirt with the old widowers on Tuesday nights. If you think the birds and bees give two hoots about getting older, you're mistaken. It's just that the bees' stingers need a little more time to recuperate than they used to. Another reason why cutting Bingo down to once a week was a good idea, if you know what I mean.

I once had the love of my life and he was all I've ever wanted, so I couldn't tell you personally about anybody's stinger in here. But I do pay attention to the life that's going on around me. Surprisingly, there's quite a bit of it here. And lots of gossip to go along with it—all in good fun, of course. Mostly out of boredom since there isn't much more to talk about. I thought it would be good to have a discussion about something more exciting than who's seen slipping out of Margo's room in the early morning hours or what's for dinner on Sunday.

I thought a few of my favorite Bukowski pieces would be a pleasant break. Make these old-timers use their brains for a change and give us residents something interesting to carry on a real conversation about. But after the incident with the new nurse two nights ago, I was doubting myself. Bukowski might not be the best choice—not the three poems I selected anyway. He could get a little out there, be a little raw and uncomfortable and after the misunderstanding with Lurleen, I didn't need to give anybody more reason to think I was in the early "angry" stages of Alzheimer's.

"Ms. Penny, honey, you ready?" Doltha, a care partner who has a penchant for bright orange nail polish and Salem Lights, asks. I turn my head towards her as she pushes me towards the steps of the stage set up in the corner of the dayroom. I start to reply but realize that she doesn't care one bit about what I have to say. The syrupy sweetness in her voice, too loud and overly cheerful, doesn't match the uninterested look on her face. It's obvious she'll go for a smoke break without hearing one word of old Henry or anything else from me.

The tip of my shoe catches on the edge of the top step and I almost lose my balance. Wouldn't that be perfect? Bat shit crazy old Penny, falling face first in front of everyone because of her shoes. I shake my head, steady myself, and think back to that awful scene in my room two nights ago. I'd woken up to one of the night shift nurses standing at the end of my bed, which was enough to almost give me a heart attack. I'd been in the middle of a good dream when she woke me. It confused me, but when I realized she was taking the shoes off my feet, I went from confusion to feeling violated to feeling enraged.

I'd lost my temper and in trying to defend my privacy—hell, my dignity—ended up on the list of residents that get talked to like toddlers and written off as lost causes.

Regardless of the gossip at the nurses' station that night, I'd not forgotten that my shoes were on my feet. That's plum pure-D stupid. I knew damn good and well they were there when I turned out the light.

If she'd asked me why I was wearing them to bed, instead of assuming I was nuts, none of this would've happened. If only she'd respected the little bit of independence I have left.

And for the record, I did not think she was a thief, nor did I accuse her of trying to steal them. Gossip spread like wildfire. By the time it made its way back to my end of the hallway, someone said I'd kicked the poor girl in the face. That I'd called her a thieving twat of all things. How embarrassing and completely untrue. I would never kick anyone, especially in the face, and I have never called anyone a thieving anything. Except for maybe our current President, but that's neither here nor there—I mean, honestly, who would want these old shoes but me? And I do want them, very much. I'm not insane, I'm an eighty-seven-year-old woman living in a nursing home who wants to sleep with my shoes on in peace.

I can't help but chuckle at how that sounds once I put it to words, and the chuckle turns into a laugh. No wonder they're talking about me. The last thought brings me back to the present and I make a decision. Bukowski will have to wait for another day.

I walk past the chair set out for me to the front of the platform and carefully lower myself so I'm eye level with everyone, paying close attention not to tumble over the edge. I sit down, hang my legs off the side and hear my joints pop and crack. There was a time I would have hopped to the floor below without a second thought of broken hips, ankles, or knee replacements. But I know how my body has aged even if I'm still the same on the inside. All anyone sees now is a little old woman and it changes their perception. Why years ago, my short fuse was a part of me the same as the freckles on my skin. I could pitch a good fit and never have it held over my head, it was expected of me because of my red hair. But once my hair turned white, that changed. No one here knows the girl I used to be.

All they know is an eighty-seven-year-old widow of a preacher's son—especially one that was raised in the south—ought not cuss and carry on like I do.

If they only knew the real me and not this illusion they've created. I take a deep breath and jump in with both feet.

"What's with the shoes, you ask?"

I raise my eyebrows and look into the eyes of the people sitting in the folding chairs in the first two rows. Then I acknowledge the others in their wheelchairs either pushed off to the side or in the back of the room. Everyone's quiet, ready for the scoop. It's hard to tell if Joan is leaning forward to hear me or if the strap around her waist needs to be tightened, but it's obvious she's interested in what I have to say. I can tell by the way she twists the corner of her throw. She hasn't spoken a word since she had a stroke last month, but when she's concentrating on something, she'll damn near tie a knot in her afghan. And right now, it looks like she's working a braid down the side of it.

I sit up a little straighter when I see that even Doltha has stopped at the door leading out to the patio, pack of cigarettes in hand, to hear what I have to say.

"I'll tell you about the shoes, but first I want to tell you a story. These days I hardly recognize myself when I look in the mirror. I'm always startled by the reflection staring back at me. Maybe some of you feel the same way, or maybe it's just me. But it's hard to believe that my eyes used to be as bright as the summer sky or as green as fresh-cut grass depending on the mood I was in. Or that my hair was once the color of a new copper penny.

"Now I'm as plain as a Mennonite's bonnet. Well, except for these red shoes I'm wearing that make me look a little crazy. Not scary crazy, more like the cat woman in every neighborhood kind of crazy. You know her, with her fifty half-feral felines, a carton of Camels tucked under one arm? Always has hot pink rouge applied in lopsided circles on her cheeks. Yes, I'm aware of how odd they must look on my tired feet. But then I smile at my reflection in the mirror and see a hint of the girl I was expecting to see. She's still there in the corner of my eye and that makes me feel better.

"Eyes, now those are funny organs. They're considered organs, aren't they? Always changing—needing help to see far off, and then help to see up close. Changing color like a chameleon until one day they get cloudy and stay that way. Peculiar little things they are." I feel myself wandering off the subject. But Margo and Elliot laugh and it's exactly what I need to get back on track. "Now, Jonathan's eyes were something special. Black as coal and as steady as a glass cutter. I don't recollect his ever changing. They always shined at me so's to make butterflies gather in my stomach. Lord, he still had me crazy for him years after we'd taken our vows. He was something else, that husband of mine.

"When I first met Jonathan, he was a card-carrying, bible-thumping, soapbox-standing member of the Church of Christ. The one right there on Main Street.

His daddy was the preacher there as a matter of fact, and it bothered him I wasn't a regular at the church on the corner. You know, that was unheard of back then. Well, hell, everyone but the drunkest of drunks or the wildest of sinners attended some kind of church. That's why my parents didn't go."

Esther, Rueben, and Jane laugh, and Frances nods from her wheelchair in the back of the room.

"Truth be told, my mother didn't go because she didn't need to. And my father—well, my father worked six days a week at the mill and Sunday was the only day he had to tend to his garden. He loved his roses and he loved us even more. He said the big guy in the sky wouldn't mind if we skipped the ceremony as long as we lived in his image. And we followed his rules. I don't mean those Ten Rules that people are always screwing with to suit themselves either. Treat everybody like you want them to treat you. Don't be selfish. Be nice. Plain and simple. Not going to church never felt wrong to me. My mother and father were the most loving and giving people there ever were. They treated everybody with respect.

"Well, once Jonathan took an interest in me, he thought it was his duty to get me to become a member of the church. I went with him once, only once, and said I'd never go back.

"How could I stand there and act like I belonged to

a congregation that didn't believe in music? Hell, that was the craziest thing I'd ever heard. I was young—I had to dance. Those people were insane if they thought I could stand still the rest of my life. No, ma'am. We Finley's were the dancing kind. I grew up listening to the radio with my parents. I fell asleep many a night watching them dance in the living room, my father carrying me to bed with the music still playing. If those judgmental, holier than thou people didn't think that was a spiritual experience, then they didn't know their asses from their elbows."

I make a snorting noise before I can stop myself. I'm afraid I've offended some of the more religious members of the group. But then Frances throws in an "Amen to that, sister!" so I pick up where I left off.

"Nights when my parents felt like dancing, it filled our house with so much love that you knew life was good and everything made sense. Believe in a religion where they take that away? No, thank you. As far as I was concerned, Jonathan could take his dark eyes and fix their gaze on someone else. Someone who wanted to live a boring, dance-free life. Not me. No, ma'am. Hell, we cain't all be saints.

"I guess he thought I'd come around, because he didn't give up on me that easy. One night soon after that first trip to the church, Jonathan came over for dinner. My mother was singing along with the radio in the kitchen. We sat in the living room and listened to her voice coming from the dining room as she set the table. She was singing with Hank Williams and her voice sounded like an angel's. I giggled as Jonathan squirmed when she got to the part that described how unconcerned the gal in the song was with her kind of lovin'. You know the song I'm talking about," I say and know they do by the giggles I get in reply, "he tried hard to act like he couldn't hear her, but Mama loved that song and she always sang too loud to it.

"He was so cute with those dimples stuck deep into his bright red face, you could hardly stand to look at him. I can tell by the smiles on y'alls faces you know exactly what I'm talking about. You could tell he was uncomfortable with my mama singing that song, but he never made one snarky comment. I should've felt bad but figured he owed me that much for making me go to church with him.

"I think he'd been planning on asking my parents to join him the following Sunday—maybe he thought if we all went to the church together it would make sense to us or something. But whatever his plan was, he never brought it up. My parents nipped that idea in the bud without even knowing they were doing it.

"My father asked my mother about one of our neighbors as he helped himself to the potatoes, 'Did you go by Mr. Truman's house today, dear?'

"'Yes, I did. He said to thank you for the magazines. I told him I was making a pot roast today, his favorite. He actually sounded like he was looking forward to dinner tomorrow. Poor thing, he doesn't have much of an appetite anymore.'

"Mr. Truman had cancer. He was an old widower that lived down the street. He used to come over for dinner, but he'd gotten so sick that my mother started taking meals over to him instead. She just added that little task to all the other things she did for everybody. Like walking Mrs. Thompson's poodle for her while her ankle was mending after Mrs. Thompson sprained it on a root in the sidewalk or stopping by Ms. Linda's to rock her newborn so she could take a bath or run to the grocery store. My mother was the most thoughtful, giving person I've ever met. She was damn near perfect.

"My father had asked Jonathan if he wanted to say grace, which made me giggle because we never said grace—when there was a knock on the back door. My father got up to see who it was. It was Roger, the little boy who lived across the street. His father had been gone for about a year and his mother—well, we weren't really sure what she did or where she went. But we knew Roger spent a lot of time alone. We heard him say something about a bicycle chain—his excuse for coming over this time—and then the sound of the back door closing.

"'Hey, everybody look who's here,' my father said in his loud, easy voice. 'Roger stopped by to borrow some tools. Here,' my father pulled up a chair as my mother went to the kitchen for another plate, 'have a seat. I hope you're hungry because Rosie made enough to feed the whole neighborhood.'

"Roger grinned at my dad and sat down in his usual spot. He was a regular at our house, especially on Friday nights. He was so skinny, he looked like he'd break if you hugged him too hard, which led me to believe that the dinners at our house were the only home-cooked meals he got.

"My father introduced Roger to Jonathan like he was an adult instead of a dirty-faced thirteen-year-old. I saw the look on Jonathan's face and knew he got the picture. My parents were the real deal. They didn't have to go stand in that church every Sunday to prove it. And they couldn't care less what people thought of them for not going.

"Instead of asking my parents to come to the church that night, Jonathan asked them for my hand in marriage

66

two months later. We had a small service at his daddy's church to appease his family, but after we said I do, we went on over to the American Legion and had ourselves a party. Boy howdy, did we dance on our wedding night. We danced until we both had blisters on our heels, and when we couldn't take it any longer, we kicked off our shoes and danced barefoot. Jonathan turned out to be a natural, believe it or not. I was as surprised as anyone when he taught me or thing or two on the dance floor."

I laugh and look at Margo. She knows what I'm talking about.

"That man was one in a million. We danced, my goodness, most every day of our life after that, and we had close to fifty wonderful years together. Who would have thought it, that he'd fall for a red-headed heathen like me?"

I have to stop and shake my head at this part, and it's not for effect. It still amazes me that Jonathan picked me when he could have had any girl in the state. Me with my freckles and my fondness for four-letter words. Me— Penelope Maitilde Finley. The girl with the crazy orange hair and tacky red shoes. The sound of Doltha's chair scooting closer brings me back to the present. I can't believe she changed her mind about the extra smoke break. I thought for sure she'd be outside puffing away and playing a mind-numbing game of solitaire on her phone. But instead, she's with the residents, wiping her eyes with a Kleenex, sitting on the edge of her chair. I look around and realize that everyone is paying attention. Even Thaddeus, who is only quiet when reruns of Bonanza are playing on the big screen in the TV room or he's sleeping, is leaning forward. His mouth shut and his eyes open. I clear my throat and continue. "I know he loved me as much as I loved him. And, honey, I couldn't have loved that man any more than I did. He was my world. Jonathan didn't want to leave me any more than I wanted him to go. But that's life and we don't get to pick the way it ends.

"I was there when he passed, what—ten years ago now? He smiled at me—I swear he did. He smiled and said, 'It's time, Penny. I love you.' And he squeezed my hand. I started to cry, and he said, 'Don't you cry now, sweetheart. No crying. We will be together again, and you better wear your dancing shoes because I hear music.' Then he closed his eyes. And that was that."

I straighten my back and rock slightly from side to side, suddenly aware of how hard the stage is on my bony behind. I stretch forward, looking down at my shoes and kick my legs back and forth to get circulation going in them again. Plus, I need a minute to keep the tears that have sprung up from running down my cheeks. When I'm sure I've got them under control I look up at the group.

"So that's why I wear these shoes. They're the first thing I put on after I shower, yep, the very first. Even before my step-ins," I thought that would get at least a chuckle, but I'm the only one laughing. I take a deep breath to finish my story. If they remember anything of what I say, I want it to be this last part.

"Shoot, y'all, as old as I am, my number could be called any damn minute. I don't know when my ticket will be punched. Jonathan said to wear my dancing shoes, so I wear them every day. Yes, it's true that I sleep in them. It would be crazy not to. I have to be prepared, don't I?

"One thing I'm sure of—even if I don't know anything else about what happens in this life or after we die—is this. Jonathan and I are going to have one hell of a first dance on the other side of the veil."

Jimmy

*"All the stuff I'd been thinking was swirling around
in my head. I wanted to tell her everything."*

Whew, it's going to be another scorcher. By ten
o'clock this morning the black dial on the thermometer
pointed to ninety-eight degrees. But the heat doesn't
bother me. It gives me an excuse to roll open the big
metal doors and turn on the floor fans in the garage. It's
kind of nice actually, you can't hear all the bullshit that
runs rampant over the roar of those huge commercial
fans. I'm not one for small talk and gossip like my
mechanics and the regular customers that like to hang out
here. It doesn't seem to matter that I own this place,

people still come here talking a bunch of nonsense. But since I do own it, I can turn on all the fans and roll up the doors no matter what the temperature is outside. I even turn on the air compressor, whether I need it or not, when the bullshit starts getting a little too deep. It makes enough racket to shut Gene up, the self-appointed town crier, before he's repeated the same story twice—and that's saying a lot.

I'm officially closed for the day but staying to work on one of Mr. Pruitt's trucks. He thinks I'm doing him a big favor by staying after closing time, but truth be told, I like working after everyone else has gone. It gives me a chance to clear my mind. The shop is a different place once the "open" sign has been turned over to "closed" and the pumps have been shut off. I waved goodbye to Steve about an hour ago, but I'll still pay him for a solid eight hours. The kid is a genius when it comes to working on engines, but not so much when it comes to relationships. He has a new girlfriend and can't seem to get out of here early enough. I figure that'll last for another month or so—three months at the longest. That won't change until he starts noticing girls for more than their dancing skills, if you get my drift. I've never understood why he keeps making the same choices—except for the obvious reasons, of course. But hell, just like my older brother used to say, titties is titties. Every girl he falls for finds someone new when the new wears off and Steve's out of money. You'd think he'd learn, but he just finds another stripper to fall in love with down at the club. Poor kid.

I guess—no, *I know* I am a lucky man. Aida and me have been married for close to twenty years now and I'm as crazy about her as I was thirty years ago. She's still as pretty as the first day I saw her, even more so. Maybe not as sweet, but damn close. She's a great cook, and keeps house better than my own mother did, but it's more than that. She's more than that. Aida's got gumption. She's tough. She's a loyal friend, and one of the best damn poker players I've ever sat across a table from. She volunteers at the nursery at our church more than anybody else there and we don't even have kids. She loves the babies, that's why she does it—I also know that's the only reason she goes to church, whether she'll admit it or not.

I'll never forget the first time I saw her. It was a day like today, another hot southern scorcher. Aida was picking blackberries by what we thought was our secret swimming hole. Me and the boys were skinny dipping, but she didn't know we were there. I just about died when I looked up and saw her standing up on the bank slightly above us. I was hoping we could hide until she left, but loudmouth Jeffrey thought it'd be funny to mess with her. Try to embarrass her. He wanted to send her back home crying, you could see it in his eyes. He swam right up to the bank before any of us had time to do anything about it. I was ashamed.

I couldn't believe even he would do something so lowdown. I knew I should do something, but I was buck naked and at a loss. Even if I'd had swimming trunks on, I didn't want her to know I was there, that I was friends with someone like Jeffrey.

She was so busy trying to not get caught in the briars—or maybe she was watching out for snakes—whatever the reason, she didn't notice him until he was right up on her.

Jeffrey, feeling full of himself and putting on a show, stood up in the shallow water and called her name. I couldn't see his face, just his tan shoulders and white cheeks, but I saw hers when she turned around.

It was right then that this twelve-year-old boy fell in love.

Aida looked shocked for a split second, then she raised her hand up as if to shield the sun from her eyes. She squinted at Jeffrey's pecker, looked around at our heads bobbing in the deep end, then back at Jeffrey in all his fourteen-year-old glory. She took a deep breath, leaned slightly forward like she was giving him a thorough inspection and said loud and clear—loud enough for us all to hear, "Well damn, Jeffrey Sneed. How do you expect to catch any fish with that little worm? That's the most pitiful bait I ever seen."

With that, she turned around and started walking— fast, but not *running*—up the well-worn path to the road. When she got to the top, she turned around and spied our clothes tossed carelessly under a low pine branch off to the side of the path. I held my breath until she took a few steps past them, but then she glanced back over her shoulder.

Jeffrey was still standing there, trying to act like he hadn't heard her. But we knew better. Hell, the whole town probably heard her. Like I said, she was *loud* and *clear*. If we hadn't all been so shocked at her response, we'd have laughed our asses off.

I don't know if the fact that he had the balls— regardless of the size—to still be standing there pissed her off. It didn't cross my mind until later that she could've been downright scared he might chase after her, but whatever it was that spurred her, she threw down her bucket with enough force to send berries flying back to the water's edge. Before we had time to know what was happening, she darted off the path and grabbed all of our clothes in one clean sweep. Then she was out of there like a shot. I'd never seen a girl, or boy for that matter, run so fast

I should tell Aida how proud of her I was that day.

We waited until the sun went down, shriveled and water-logged, before we took off for Ron's place to borrow some clothes. It wasn't a good plan, since Ron was a foot shorter and twenty pounds lighter than all of us, but his house was the closest.

We were trying to figure out how we were going to make the trip without being on the road naked. The only other option was to take our chances climbing over several barbed wire fences—dangling and in the dark— when we stumbled over our clothes in the ditch a few feet away. We thanked our lucky stars, grabbed our clothes, put them on as fast as possible and took off towards our separate homes.

I went back to our not so secret swimming hole the next day by myself. I was thinking of Aida. I was hoping that she would be there, and I could apologize to her for not standing up for her. She wasn't there, but I found her bucket still on the path where she threw it down. The berries flattened by our feet from the day before made me feel ashamed all over again. I picked up the bucket and filled it to the brim with blackberries and took it to her house.

I wanted to knock on the door but didn't have the courage. I stood there a minute or two, thinking about what I'd say if she stepped out onto the porch, but decided to leave the bucket there for her to find. I later learned—at our wedding reception to be exact—that her dad had seen me out on the porch too nervous to knock. Shuffling my feet and talking to myself. She'd not told him about the incident at the creek, so he'd gotten it all wrong.

Aida never corrected him because she said she liked her dad's story better anyway. He mentioned it in his toast to us, and it was one of his favorite stories to tell when he got so old he couldn't remember what day it was. He never forgot the story of *"the little shy feller who was so smitten with his Aida he courted her with blackberries."* He told it many times over the years and I'm damn thankful we never told him any different.

* * *

I heard a noise out front that brought me out of my thoughts. I stuck my head around the office door so I could see through the big windows that looked out over the parking lot. I spied Kenny, Lester Farley's boy, at the soda machine. He was struggling to pull his Coke from the machine when he saw me and waved. I waved back. He was a good kid—a big football playing, tobacco farming, God-fearing Robertson County boy. I thought to myself, like I had a thousand times before, how it'd be nice to have a couple of sons like that. Me and Aida never have had any kids of our own. There was that one time when we thought it was going to happen, but I guess it just wasn't meant to be.

I watched Kenny walk back to his four-wheel drive and laughed to myself when I noticed he'd already downed half of the bottle.

Aida's dad loved his Cokes, too. I'd use them as an excuse to stop by and check on him there at the end, take him a Coke and stay and watch the late-night news with him. He'd turned into a night owl in his old age and spent most nights in the comfortable recliner in his living room with a book long after everyone else was in bed. Some nights I had a hard time sleeping myself, so it worked out good for both of us.

After his wife left him, Aida tried to her best to coax him into moving in with us, but he never would do it. Even though he ate dinner at our house most every night, he never gave in to Aida's pleas to sell his house. We never pushed him hard on the subject, and I'm glad we didn't. He liked his house and he liked his time alone. I understood completely. It was one of the saddest days of my life when he passed. It was a Tuesday night—I don't know why I remember that, but I do—when I went to check on him, taking his bottle of Coke as usual. I called his name from the porch, but he didn't answer. I wasn't surprised, since his hearing wasn't as good as it used to be, so I let myself in through the unlocked screen door into the kitchen. I put some ice in a glass and filled it halfway with his Coke, stopping to get two ripe bananas out of a bowl of fruit on the counter for us to eat while we watched the ten o'clock news. He was sitting in his recliner, a well-worn copy of his favorite James Lee Burke novel in his lap.

At first, I'd thought he was taking a catnap, but then I noticed that he didn't look right. Before I ever touched him, I knew he wasn't breathing. He was gone. When I took his hand in mine, it was cold, but I held it anyway. I cried like I didn't know I could, a deep, painful, cry for this man who had been like a father to me. More than a father, he was my friend.

Once I got control of myself, I called an ambulance. But I waited until I heard the siren in the distance before I called Aida. I knew she would take it hard and I didn't want her to see him like that—a shell—and I knew he wouldn't want it either. Plus, I didn't want her to hear me crying. I felt that she would need me to be strong for her, so I waited until I was sure I had my emotions under control. I never told her how I cried for an hour before I called the ambulance.

Whew, what a funeral. It was a sad one. His death was a shock to everyone. He'd been so strong and independent. His sudden passing caused his friends to question their mortality it seemed, and they were a pitiful lot.

Aida, being Aida, spent most of the service trying to lift everyone's spirits. Her mother had remarried several times since the divorce and was on a cruise ship somewhere with her sixth or seventh husband on the day Aida's dad died. I don't know if she would've come to the funeral anyway; too busy polishing her jewelry and planning her next wedding to think about her daughter's feelings, so Aida and I took care of all the details. He didn't have any family left but Aida. And me, I reckon.

* * *

The familiar click of the answering machine brought me out of my thoughts. I'd gone so far down the rabbit hole chasing old memories I hadn't heard the phone ring. I put down the socket wrench and leaned toward the office door to hear the message. Aida's voice filled the quiet space. Like a lifeline, her voice pulled me back into the present.

"I guess you're working hard, so I'm going to go ahead and eat without you. I'll put your plate in the oven to keep it warm, okay? Oh, I picked some pretty tomatoes today, so check the fridge—I sliced you some big fat pieces just like you like them. Don't forget them, they're perfect. Well...

okay, I love you."

She stopped to take a breath. "And don't worry about waking me up when you come in, no matter how late it is. I don't have a thing to do tomorrow ..." BEEP. The time had run out. She wouldn't call back. Believe it or not, as much as she liked to talk—and Aida could talk the ears off the Easter Bunny—she wasn't much for talking on the phone. No, she'd rather talk face to face.

Like the time she came down here to the station with her big news. I was working under somebody's car at the time, but the sight of her caught my eye. Lying on my back she appeared to be upside down, running up the middle of the road with her hair pulled back in a rubber band and her cheeks flushed pink, she looked like a schoolgirl. She ran into the office first, then out to the garage and pulled me out from under the car by my ankles. She leaned over me and laughed out loud. Then she started crying. I sat up on the rolling cart, but she pushed me back down and started laughing again.

"Woman, what is wrong with you?" I remember asking her. She scared me a little bit. I'd seen crazy before and this looked a little too familiar.

"Ain't nothing wrong with me, Mr. Chance. Nothing that'll last longer than nine months, anyways." She beamed down at me. I am not a dumb man, but it didn't sink in right away. She took my hand and put a white plastic stick in it that had a blue plus sign on one end. I didn't say I was smart—just not dumb. I still didn't get it. She beamed even brighter.

That's when she said the magic words, "I hope he gets his smarts from me—I'm pregnant, dim bulb!"

I stood up so quick I sent the cart flying across the garage floor. I grabbed Aida and picked her up off her feet. I swung her around and around and said something goofy like, "I do hope she has your brains and my looks." The next thing I knew, we were home, making love like there was no tomorrow. I just went and left the station wide open—didn't even lock the cash register. That was back before I'd hired anybody else to help out at the garage. Lucky for us, Gene, the town gossip, had been at the pharmacy and spied Aida buying the pregnancy test. When he stopped by to see if I'd heard anything and noticed me gone, he figured he'd stick around to get the full story. About five hours later, when I realized what I'd done, I came in to lock up and he was still there waiting. Hell, he'd even pumped a few gallons of gas in the meantime.

Those were the happiest five months of my life. I wanted that baby more than I'd ever wanted anything in my life. I pictured a little girl with dark curls and freckles. I'd take her fishing on Saturdays and to the high school ballgames on Friday nights. I'd tell her stories about her mama's daddy and make up happy ones for her about mine. I'd keep all the bad things away from her and she'd never want for nothing. I'd teach her how to rebuild a carburetor and how to listen when people talked. You know, the important stuff.

Every night Aida and I stayed up way past our bedtime making plans.

Then one night I woke up to Aida whimpering. I was having a bad dream and thought it was in my head at first, but it didn't take but a second to realize that the sounds were coming from her and not a dream. She was trying to get up to go to the bathroom, but she was in pain and couldn't stand up straight. I got up to help her and saw the blood on the back of her gown. I wrapped her in the bed sheet so she wouldn't see it while I tried to figure out what to do, but she knew something was wrong. She ripped back the sheet, saw the blood, and begged me to help her. I told her I would, and she trusted me. I stayed strong. I called her doctor and told him we were on our way to the hospital. I stayed calm; even though on the inside I was panicking. I got her there in five minutes flat and carried her in the emergency entrance just like I'd carried her across the threshold on our wedding night, but this time we weren't laughing.

The doctors weren't able to do anything to save our

baby. They did their best to assure us that we hadn't done anything wrong, but that didn't help ease the pain. They gave Aida something to make her sleep and let nature take its course. I cried so hard that night my stomach ached for days afterwards, but I made sure I was finished with the tears before Aida woke up.

I figured the last thing she needed was to see me crying and helpless.

After that, Aida's doctor told us that the chances of us getting pregnant again were slim. I just didn't believe it. They didn't know Aida like I did. They didn't know how determined she could be. I tried to convey this to her, but it hurt Aida too much to talk about. She needed time to heal. So, I quit talking about it for a while and then I couldn't find the right way to start the conversation again. Aida never brought it up, so we quit talking about it all together.

It never made any sense to me. Why would our baby be taken away before it even got here? It never had a chance, not even a minute, why would that happen? I'll never be able to wrap my head around that, and I guess I'm not supposed to. There have been other things that have happened in my life that I've not understood, but when I think about our baby… I don't know. It's true that death is part of living, I get that. I've seen enough of it to understand that it is inevitable—but our baby?

Before she was even born? It just makes no sense.

Like when my brother died. We were playing in the treehouse just like we'd done so many days before. It was me, Ron, and my brother, Adam. I remember that day just like it was yesterday.

Adam was going to swing from the doorway of the treehouse to a limb in the tree next to us. We thought he was crazy; the rope was too short, and the limb was too skinny. We thought the worst thing that could happen to Adam was blistered fingers from rope burn. Ron and I were laughing at him for even thinking it was possible, and he was being goofy, taking bets even though he knew he couldn't make it. Adam laughing with us. The sound of his laugh turning into a surprised yelp when he fell. Just slipped backwards through the open doorway. He never touched the ground.

Somehow, the rope had gotten wrapped around his neck in the fall. Adam was dead before we made it down the ladder. He was thirteen. I was ten.

Telling my dad … the funeral … everything was a blur. The only thing I can remember much about my brother's death is my dad burning down the tree after Adam's funeral. Well, actually just the treehouse, somehow the tree made it.

I woke up to see flames outside my bedroom

window and I thought the house was on fire. I ran downstairs to my parents' room and their bed was empty. I ran out the side door and tripped over my mother, barely caught myself before I fell headfirst onto the sidewalk, but she never felt me. She was sitting on the top step staring up at the sky but not seeing anything. She looked like she was asleep with her eyes open. It was the scariest thing I'd ever seen in my life—even worse than the look in Adam's eyes when Ron and I got to the bottom of the ladder. The light was gone in Adam's eyes, but my mother's eyes were unnaturally bright, they looked like two lasers or something no longer human.

I heard my dad yell and ran around the side of the house expecting to find him on fire by the noise he was making. The words, s*top, drop and roll,* stuck in the back of my throat when I found him. He held a half-empty bottle of Johnny Walker Red in one hand and a can of gasoline in the other one. I forgot about the fire as I listened to my father yell at God for taking his *good* son. He was screaming like a crazy man and slinging gasoline everywhere. Screaming and cursing and not making any sense at all.

It had never been a secret that Adam was his favorite. Adam was the spitting image of our father, only a happy, nice version of the man he was named after. I was my mother's baby, a carbon copy of her older brother who she adored. He'd died in the war and my father hated him for it. My father had some kind of condition, which was never discussed, that kept him from joining the army with all of his buddies. That wasn't the first or last time he felt discriminated against, but it was the thing that bothered him the most. He thought everyone was always against him. He was jealous of Robert for being a war hero, and he was jealous of me for looking like someone my mother worshipped. He hated that I didn't look anything like him. I'd heard him say several times that he wasn't even sure I was his—which was ridiculous. My mother was a proud southern Christian lady who would never think about breaking her vows. Not even to save herself.

I cried out when I saw the treehouse engulfed in flames. Adam and me had everything stashed up there. My baseball cards and Adam's catcher's mitt, Hot Wheel cars, and a girlie magazine Adam had nicked from somewhere—my brother's prize possession. All of my comic books, our geode collection. Everything sacred was in that treehouse, and everything was gone. That was our safe place, where we'd go to get away from the old man. My father heard me cry out.

When he turned towards me, dropping the bottle of scotch to remove his belt singlehandedly, I was too grief-stricken to do anything but stand there. Where would I have gone anyway? My brother—my protector and best friend—was gone. My hiding place was burning to ashes right in front of my eyes. My mother was sitting on the porch, but she wasn't there, and might not ever come back. I felt like a rabbit caught in a trap, waiting to be put out of my misery. My father was still swinging his belt, the buckle hitting me hard enough to cut, when the firemen got there.

I never told anybody, but I was sure I was going to be burned alive that night. Before the fireman got there, my father had soaked my pajamas with gasoline. Lucky for me, he dropped his lighter. When he was searching on the ground for his cigarette lighter, I came to my senses and tried to run away. He gave up on setting me on fire and tried to beat me to death instead.

It took two firemen to pull him off of me. Everyone was so busy with the fire and the two devastated adults, that no one noticed me when I ran inside and locked myself in my bedroom. No one ever came to check on me. Not that night, or any night after.

Everyone heard about the fire, that he'd burned down the treehouse. A lot of people thought it made perfect sense, seeing as how Adam had died. But no one knew that was the night my mother turned into a zombie and my dad completely lost his mind. The night he almost killed me.

Our neighbors tried to treat my parents the same after the funeral, but no one knew what to do or say. My mother hardly ever spoke after that, to me or anyone else. I know she didn't stop loving me, she just couldn't show me anymore. It was all she could do to get out of bed each day. And my dad tried his best to ignore me, except to punish me if I came home late, or didn't get my chores done fast enough. It was like he was scared of what he might do if he was left alone with me for too long at a time.

* * *

A cramp in my side brought me out of my thoughts. I stood up and stretched, counting the pops in my back; the muscles in my neck and shoulders pretty tense. Funny, I never noticed the odor of gasoline in my own garage—which is ridiculous. It is a *gas* station after all, but it doesn't bother me except when I let my mind wander back to that summer. Then it's all I can smell. Suddenly the stench was so strong I couldn't stand it. I rolled up one of the doors and turned on a fan. I went into the office and got a beer out of the dinged-up apartment sized refrigerator under the counter. I drank it there, standing at the counter, waiting for the garage to air out. I finished, got another one, and walked back to Mr. Pruitt's truck.

I ran my thumb across the label on the bottle and had to smile. Miller High Life, or as we used to call it, the cream soda of beers. I had my first one with Ron when we turned seventeen. That's when we started making plans to get out of town, to make our escape. Like so many other boys our age, we joined the army as soon as we turned eighteen. I was taught and saw things I've spent years trying to forget.

No matter how hard I tried to fit in as a soldier, I just wasn't made for the army. As soon as my two years was up, I moved back to my hometown. Ron re-upped, was made General after a while, and today he's some kind of big shot in Asheville. We keep in touch and I still consider him one of my closest friends. As much as I'd hated my time in the service, I'd planned on re-upping when my first term was over. I still didn't know what I wanted to do, I knew I couldn't go back and watch my mother continue to put up with my father's abuse, but I wasn't ready to leave home—the only home I'd ever known—permanently. It turned out that the decision was made for me.

My mother and father were the victims of a head-on collision. My mother was killed instantly. I've always been grateful for that, that she didn't have to suffer any more than she already had.

My father wasn't so lucky. He was paralyzed from the neck down and was a resident of Quiet Acres Nursing Home—ironic seeing as how it was anything but quiet there—until he died a few years later. Everyone thought I moved back to be close to him, so I could visit him and make sure he was treated the way he should be treated, which I did. Visit him, that is. I made sure he was treated fairly humanely. Not the way he should be treated.

But the main reason I moved back home was because of that tough little girl I'd met out at the swimming hole.

I'd never forgotten the look on her face, or the way she was determined not to let Jeffrey get the best of her. I knew she was something special. I'd never met another girl like Aida. She came with her father to my mother's funeral and I knew that she was the one I wanted to spend my life with. I told her how I felt on our very first date, which didn't happen until a year after I came back; and might not have happened then if Aida hadn't asked me what was taking me so long to ask her out. We were married one month later.

I need to tell her again—and I will. I'll tell her as soon as I go home tonight. I think I'll tell her how I still dream about our little girl. How I believe that Aida would be the best mother and grandmother in the whole state of

Tennessee. Maybe it's time we talked about checking into adopting a baby, or we could see about becoming foster parents—or, hell, go to a real specialist somewhere and let them have a look at what's going on in there. I read about stranger things happening in the paper every day. I want to tell her how sometimes I imagine I can see my mother holding our little girl on the other side. I don't know if it's heaven exactly, or just on the other side of a curtain or veil or—hell, I don't know. I've never talked to anybody about anything like that before. But I don't think it's too much to believe that they are waiting for us, and my mother is her beautiful, whole self again. I want to run that by her and see what she thinks.

I'll tell her about the bad dreams I have, where Adam falls over and over. Some nights she wakes me and tells me I'm talking in my sleep, but I've never told her why. I've never talked to her about the dreams. I think tonight I finally will.

I'll tell her all these things that I think about when I'm here working by myself without anyone to disturb my thoughts. All these things that I hold inside and never say out loud to anyone.

* * *

"Do you know what time it is, Jimmy? It is eleven o'clock, I was starting to get worried ..." Aida's voice still sounds so young. I realize how quiet the garage is, she must have turned off the fan and I hadn't even noticed. "I brought you some dinner, I thought you might be hungry. It's your favorite."

I look up from under the hood and find Aida standing there in one of my old flannel shirts. She looks like she's been sleeping, her hair pulled up in an uneven ponytail and eyes slightly puffy. If I tell her how beautiful she is right now, she'll roll her eyes and shake her head. Think I'm teasing. Because she has no idea how perfect she is.

When our eyes meet, she smiles. I feel tears come to my eyes and turn away. I pretend to put my tools up. She's still talking, God love her. She talks enough for the both of us.

"...I hope it's still warm. If not, we can pop it in the microwave. Jimmy, are you even listening to me? You were in another world when I came in. You didn't even know I was here. I stood there talking for a good five minutes before you ever turned around. Lord, I wish I knew what was going on in there." She points at my head. "What were you thinking about, anyway?"

I stand there looking at this woman who I love so much it almost hurts. I reach for her and pull her close to me, nearly knocking the plate of meatloaf out of her hand. She leans back, smiles, and looks up into my face.

All the stuff I'd been thinking was swirling around in my head. I want to tell her everything, all of it. I feel my heart swell to twice its size. I feel my jaw tighten and the creases form in the corner of my mouth, the look that gets mistaken for a shit-eating grin but is really there from years of biting my tongue.

I'm afraid I might tear up. Afraid I'll scare Aida if she sees me cry, and I'm afraid I won't be able to stop once I start. So I stop myself before that happens and I hear myself say the only thing I can. My standard answer.

"Oh, nothin' much."

Sanctify

"... she wondered which one of them would be freed first."

Vernon Messiah Jackson Jr. took a deep breath, expanding his chest as much as the seams and buttons of his shirt would allow. He leaned over the pulpit for effect.

"SANC-tify!" Spit flew from his mouth as he shouted once more. Vernon Jackson was a big man, and he held the bible in his hand like it was locked and loaded.

The people of the congregation revered him. They were caught up in his spirit, his passion in the word, in his zeal to save them from the other side. Vernon held them all in the palm of his hand. Each one of his sisters and brothers were convinced that he was talking to them personally.

They emptied their pockets and change purses gladly when the offering plates were passed, no one wanted to be left behind on judgment day. And no one wanted Vernon to come to their house for a visit regarding that week's tithes or more to the point, the lack of.

"Amen, brother!"

"Testify!"

"Hallelujah!"

They shouted from the pews, hands waving above their heads, so glad to have someone like him to fight the good fight for their souls. What a strong man, they'd say. What a good God-fearing man to lead them, they'd say. No one wanted a man like that against them, they thought.

"SANCTIFY yourself in the Lord!" He thrust his hand toward the room but pointed his finger at the only person he was looking at, the one he'd been eyeing since he started the sermon. He pointed as steady and threatening as the barrel of a gun towards a thin, weary-looking woman in the front pew.

His wife. There were two boys at her side, his pride and joy.

He wanted a third.

"You've got to be sanctified and show it!" He leaned back from the pulpit and dug his finger between the collar of his shirt and his neck, trying to loosen its grip on his Adam's apple. He could feel himself getting worked up, could taste the bile rising in his throat, and swallowed hard.

Marla Dowdle tilted slightly to her left and looked around the head in the pew in front of her for a better view. It looked to her like the big man standing behind the pulpit was about to "pitch a hizzy." She'd known his mama, a hard-headed and hard-working woman who stayed after her boy like a swarm of gnats until the very day she died. Many times, embarrassed by her spoiled son's behavior, she would lean over to Marla and say, "You watch, that boy's about to pitch a hizzy." And she was right. No matter what punishment he received, and his mama tried everything, he would not be tamed.

Marla knew good and well when Vernon got himself worked up. She'd seen him as a boy so wound up that he would make himself sick. Just bend right over and throw up, mad at the Little League umpire, or a chore he was asked to do that he felt beneath him.

Even though Marla missed her friend, she was grateful she wasn't around to witness the antics of her hizzy pitching son, now full grown and manipulative as ever. Marla wasn't a fan of Vernon Jackson's—of his personality or his preaching—he just happened to be the only preacher within walking distance and Marla was determined to get her steps

97

in every day, Sundays included. She glanced around at her neighbors and wondered if anyone else would admit they felt the same way. A moan, one that sounded closer to a growl, brought her attention back to the pulpit.

Vernon was sick this morning. It felt like his insides were on fire, but he would not show any signs of weakness. Whatever was going on would pass. Probably his wife's bad cooking. She was a good cook most of the time. But this morning's breakfast did not want to sit right. He regretted having that third biscuit, could feel it sitting like a rock in his gullet along with the sharp pains in his stomach.

Vernon fought the urge to unbutton his collar while taking a second to look around the room at his faithful, jittery flock of sheep. They looked to Vernon with eyes full of fear and he thrived on it. He drew from the power of the word in the Good Book and the faces of his followers and there he found the strength to ignore the pain he felt deep in his gut. And he believed Gabriel himself might be keeping him from snatching his wife up and slapping her face in front of God and everybody. He stood up straight and pulled a breath deep into his belly to get a handle on his emotions. Oh, Lord, how he'd love to slam her to the floor. He would whisper to her, "Raise your blasphemous bones off this floor. Arise and walk, or I'll step on your neck." He gritted his teeth as sweat ran from behind his ear into the fabric. There was payment to be made for her disrespectful comments this morning before breakfast.

Vernon swooned as he felt the shirt tightening enough to squeeze the air out of him. He was having trouble breathing. Every breath brought a sharp pain from his bowels to his chest and back again. He put the Bible down and held onto the stand in front of him with sweaty hands. Vernon overcame the pain and managed to take a deep breath. He needed to wrap this up and get out of here and sit down someplace. He firmly said, "Let us pray."

Everyone sitting in the pews bowed their heads and closed their eyes. Vernon kept his wide open, looking at his wife. Her head was bowed, but he could sense her lack of submission. He closed his left eye like sighting a pistol.

Vernon believed he sometimes had the gift, but erratic and undependable, and seemed to know what sinners were thinking. Something had changed in her that he couldn't put his finger on. Something small, but he would put a stop to it before she got above her raising. Like this morning, she hadn't turned loose a single tear when he punished her. She hadn't cowered to him. She had not apologized. She seemed to go inside herself and hide.

He didn't like it, not one bit.

He felt another sharp pain in his gut. This one was

followed by a feeling he didn't like, couldn't read. He felt feverish and sensed goose bumps rise up on his arms and a chill run down his back, causing him to shudder slightly. Vernon imagined he heard his mama's laughing voice whisper in his ear, "Someone walk over your grave, Little Big Man?"

In that second, he thought he saw Cora smile down at the Bible on her lap. But that wasn't likely, and he blamed his blurry vision.

It took him a minute to recall the prayer he'd selected.

No one seemed to notice the big man struggle to keep himself together.

* * *

Cora Ruth Jackson sat in the front row in a dress she had sewn herself from a pattern someone gave her years ago. It was a simple pattern—easy to sew. She had five dresses in the same style, all made from different shades of the same cheap material. She shifted slightly, wincing as the hard oak pew found the small of her back. It still ached from the bruises she got this morning.

"Sanc–*tify*!" her husband bellowed.

She would've never imagined that those soft leather shoes could hurt her in the same way his steel-toed boots hurt, but they had. They weren't even broken in. Buttery Italian leather loafers with the prettiest tassels she'd ever seen. Cora had wanted to touch them but thought her fingers might leave oily marks or something Vernon would spy. She might be simple minded, but she wasn't stupid.

"SANC-tify!" her husband yelled again. Cora didn't like his eyes stuck on her, but she knew better than to look away. It was hard to watch him when he was putting on such a show. She had learned a trick a long time ago that made it a little more sufferable. She'd learned when he would come home smelling of liquor, wanting to practice his sermons in front of her, to look at his chin—not his eyes. It was a lot better that way. The look in his eyes when he was like this, waving his bible around like a weapon, would scare even people who were baptized safe if they knew the real man.

But it didn't have the same effect on her as it used to. Maybe because Vernon was thirty years her senior and it was starting to show. His neck drooped with that old man's waddle. Strutting like a tom turkey in front of the women in the congregation with his beer belly hiding his belt in the front.

To Cora, he now looked ridiculous. Silly. But she knew better than to even let her eyes smile. Vernon hated being questioned. He detested being laughed at. He might be getting old, but he was still as strong as an ox, and his fury was dangerous.

She found herself looking at his chin instead of his eyes more often, and at the oddest times, like when she served him coffee in the mornings. Especially since she found the box of rat poison under the kitchen sink, tucked away behind the moth balls and floor cleaner. She couldn't remember the exact scene when she first mixed some into the separate sugar bowl she kept on the kitchen counter away from the greedy fingers of her two boys. But she saw clearly the picture of her hand holding the spoon that sprinkled it into his coffee this morning and every morning for the last week.

She did not for a moment worry that he might taste something off. His tongue had been whiskey-soaked for so long that he would open the sausage biscuits she'd put on his plate and coat the top of the sausage patty white with salt. He would complain she was buying cheap sausage, even though it was the same brand she'd been buying for years. He said it had no taste. She was glad his tongue had been rakedraw by hundred proof.

Out of the corner of her eye, Cora saw her oldest son, Vernon Messiah Jackson the Second, pull a piece of candy out of his pocket. She'd seen him sneak the candy out of Ms. Helen's purse when they were making their way to their seat past her on the first row. He'd stolen from the elderly lady before and lied about it. If she weren't so beat down, she would be angry. Little Vernie, as his father liked to call him, thought the world owed him. When she tried to keep a handle on her two boys, their father would put a stop to it. Her job, he told her, was to serve the males of the house. If she dared raise a hand to either of "his" boys, the father took it out on the mother tenfold. Sometimes the boys made up stories to get her in trouble, not even having the decency to leave the room when she received her punishment.

They lied for the fun of lying.

Cora reached over slowly and put her hand on Vernie's arm. She gave it a pat to let him know that she saw him and meant to let him know others might have seen him steal from the old woman's purse. Not that she was going to *do* anything.

Still, he reached out and pinched her arm between his finger and thumbnail, twisting it hard enough to break the skin. She barely flinched as she pulled her hand away. Cora wouldn't risk any quick movements that might set her husband off. She must pay attention to his sermon. She was expected to nod now and then. She nodded.

This morning she'd not ironed her husband's shirt to suit him. Even though she'd ironed it the same way as she had a thousand times before. He accused her of using too much starch causing it to cut into the soft skin at his throat. He blamed her starch for making his neck look fat, making his skin sag like an old man's. Cora had said in her defense the buttons were too tight and maybe it was time to buy some new shirts in a bigger size. She thought that was an easy enough way around the predicament because the good Lord knew Vernon loved to buy new things for himself.

The next thing she remembered she was on the floor, feeling the new loafers pounding into the small of her back. As Cora curled up against the burning blows, she caught sight of the iron still on the counter where she'd set it to cool, still hot enough to leave a blister. She squeezed her eyes shut, not wanting to give him any ideas.

Afterwards, as he gathered his Bible and took a last sip of coffee, heading for the front door, he told her she should know by now not to cause him to lose his temper. Just follow the rules, he told her. "You are a stubborn, ignorant woman! Why do you make me act this way? I don't know why I waste my time trying to teach you any different. No matter how hard I try to save you, you will end up burning in hell, just like your sass talking mama."

Vernon intended to free her from her sins.

She watched him turn up his cup and drain it, and she wondered which one of them would be freed first. Her mama had found her freedom at the end of a rope. Her sass talking had gotten her killed and put a fear in her daughter that had kept her mouth shut and her head down.

When Vernon took an interest in her, she'd barely said five words to him. The next thing she knew her childhood was over before it'd even started, and she became Vernon's wife. Her aunts had been so happy that she'd married a preacher. An older, respectable man with no children to take care of and no shameful gossip in his wake. So happy to move their orphaned niece into Vernon's house, they babbled their thanks to the good Lord above that she wouldn't end up working like a dog, cleaning houses and raising someone else's children like they had.

Their first child came soon after they were married, and Cora understood why Vernon had picked a young uneducated girl like herself. She realized that first year with Vernon there was more than one way to die. No rope needed. A woman could be dead and still iron her husband's clothes, cook his meals, serve him coffee. You could be completely dead inside while your husband rooted around on top of you, sweating and grunting like a big hog. You could be quiet as a corpse while he did things to you that no one would believe even if you found the courage to repeat them. And a dead woman would offer no hand to sons who treated her like a slave.

Then Cora woke up one morning and realized she wanted to know what it felt like to live. The night before she had this realization, Cora had had a dream. She dreamt that she was standing on the edge of a wide creek.

A dream that seemed so real, Cora could smell the wild honeysuckle that covered the creekbank and hear the clear water rushing over the stones. She wanted more than anything to put her bare feet in the creek and feel the cool water on her skin. To lie back and let the water hold her—weightless and free. Something she'd never experienced. The only thing she could compare it to would be the day she'd been baptized. But that water had been muddy and too warm, almost stagnant; she'd been afraid of water moccasins and the crowd of people waiting for her in the waist high river. Afraid that they would hold her under and forget that she was there.

The water in her dream looked clean and cool, inviting instead of threatening. Alone, she could enjoy the simple pleasure without fear. Without fear...that had never been an option for Cora, asleep or awake; ever since her mama was taken from her, her life had been a never-ending nightmare.

This gift handed to her in a dream, had awakened Cora's spirit. She *had* to feel the water on her skin.

But before she could take a step closer, Vernon pulled her from the dream with a rough pinch to her thigh as he tore at her nightgown and she woke before she reached the water's edge. Somehow, even though she was no longer dreaming, Cora heard the sound of rushing water over the noise of her husband's grunts and moans. Over the protest of the rusty springs in the mattress beneath her, the stream beckoned her, and Cora knew she would find salvation there. Like the instant turn of Saul in the Bible, she felt there was another way. Her eyes were open.

"SANCTIFY yourself in the Lord!" he shouted again, pointing at her.

Cora listened to the boys chuckling under their breath from their places on the front row. Little Vernie had started telling everyone he wanted to be a preacher, just like his daddy. The thought made her chest hurt. When she'd given birth to the last one, named Curtis after his great granddaddy, she thought there might be hope for him. He hadn't looked anything like Vernon. He'd seemed to be a happy baby, but God help her, he was meaner than his brother. Just this morning Curtis refused to eat his breakfast, called her a stupid old sow because she had overcooked the bacon.

He liked it crispy, not *crumbly.*

Vernon had cut a sideways glance toward his youngest son and said, "You have to admire a man that knows what he wants." Then laughed into his coffee cup. Cora had almost laughed with him. There was nothing funny at all in what he'd said, but the sound of his laughter echoing inside his empty cup had struck a nerve. She'd had to fight the urge to laugh by going into the kitchen and putting a dishtowel over her mouth. Cora stood there staring out the kitchen window towards her garden of scrawny tomato plants wilted in the heat. Pitiful looking things. Scorched by the relentless Tennessee summer sun, dying of thirst in the parched red clay that sold itself as soil. She knew exactly how they felt. From somewhere outside, just right past the windowsill, Cora swore she heard the sound of a running stream calling to her. Standing at the window with the dishcloth over her mouth, she'd wondered if she was going insane. The thought crossed her mind that she probably had already arrived.

She listened to her husband standing behind the pulpit, watched him gesture wildly, heard him proclaim the word "sanctify." Cora had heard this particular sermon more than once in the eleven long years they'd been married. When she first heard it, she believed in a loving and forgiving God. She trusted a God who took care of his children. But if it was her up there preaching, she'd warn everybody in the house to take care of yourself. No one else would do that for you.

Vernon screamed, "Sanctify, children!" But Cora heard another word altogether.

Sac-ri-fice!

Heard Vernon yell at her clear as a church bell. "Sacrifice! Sacrifice yourself, woman!"

From her crazy place, Cora heard an older woman's voice—a voice as clear and cool as a mountain stream—whisper in her ear, "Save yourself, child." And she knew, like the sky had parted, that she would never have to listen to another one of her husband's sermons again.

Picking Up Puppies

*"…sometimes it's harder to accept kindness
from people than it is to accept meanness. It just
depends on what you are used to."*

I knowed she was trouble as soon as she came through
the door. She couldn't have been a day over sixteen and had
to have been at least seven months along. Sashaying in,
without a speck of decency. No shame at all in the way her
short dress stretched across her round belly. She didn't even
try to hide it. Not to mention all that eye makeup. Lord, she
looked like a raccoon.

I watched her from the kitchen where I'd stepped back
to sneak a quick puff or two off my menthol. I'd officially
quit three years ago, but every once in a while—especially

on Thursdays when Clayton's bunch came in for lunch—I still needed some nicotine. Those men would cause Mother Theresa to curse. As I stood there staring through the window in the wall between the kitchen and the bar, she walked up to the counter and climbed onto a stool. No regard for the fact that her behind was barely covered as she hitched her leg onto the seat. I made a mental note to get the Lysol out from under the sink when she left.

I inhaled the last of my cigarette and took a drink of Diet Coke thinking about how much times have changed. Back in my day, if you found yourself in that "condition," you kept yourself at home, or went to visit an aunt in Kentucky. And you tried not to embarrass your parents any more than you already had. You didn't flaunt the situation in a hot pink sundress.

"What can I get you?" I asked, startling her as I came through the swinging doors.

"Uhm, a glass of milk and an order of onion rings," she said without looking up to acknowledge me. I wasn't one bit surprised by her lack of respect.

As I poured her milk into a cold beer mug from the cooler, I noticed that she was counting her change. I bet she was going to try to sneak out without paying, so I made another mental note to watch the door.

Pat was out by the dumpsters smoking half pack

of Camels, where he always went after cooking for Clayton's crew. So I put the girl's onion rings in the deep fryer for him. I didn't blame him for the break, Clayton and his golf buddies were pigs. Every time it was the same thing. They ordered two cheeseburgers apiece and a dozen orders of french fries. Complaining the whole time about the service and the amount of grease in their food, but they always came back a week later to torment us again.

I snuck another look at her to make sure she wasn't stealing a saltshaker or the napkin holder. Why, I bet she'd never cooked a meal for herself. She probably had a mama at home right now wringing her hands over her wild child, beating herself up wondering where she'd gone wrong. I could just imagine her poor mama, worrying herself sick over her unborn grandchild, while her daughter is out looking for ways to steal onion rings and—by the way she was dressed—a sugar daddy.

By the time her onion rings were ready, I'd worked myself into a tizzy thinking about that Lady DaDa, and Bridgette Spears—good lord, no wonder kids today have no respect for their parents or themselves—running around in their underwear and all. Back in my day, we didn't have that mess on TV to warp our tender minds. Even if we had, my daddy wouldn't have put up with it.

Not for a second. Why, I could've never worn a dress like that gaudy thing, pregnant or not.

I tried to calm myself as I walked back to the counter. The last thing I needed to do was have a "come to Jesus" meeting right here before our dinner rush with some sassy teenager I didn't even know.

"Here you go," I said as I handed Miss Priss her onion rings. She still didn't look at me and I felt the hairs on the back of my neck stand straight up. I was going to make her look me in the eye at least once. It wouldn't kill her to show a little respect to her elders.

"Ketchup?" I barked, more of an accusation than a question. That worked a little better than I'd intended. She— and Shelby Jean and Georgia sitting two tables over— looked at me. It was then that I noticed right away what I'd mistaken for too much eye makeup was bruises that were starting to fade. I didn't have to look twice to make sure, 'cause lord knows I'd seen them same eyes staring back at me from my own mirror.

I felt my stomach drop clear to my feet and a tightness creep across my chest. I put my hand on my heart to stop it from fluttering. Sights like that were always hard for me to ignore— looking at her face was like looking at a ghost from my past.

"Lord, don't I look a sight," she exclaimed when she

saw my shocked expression. "I ran right into my bedroom door a couple of nights ago." She paused with a funny laugh complete with a snort. It sounded genuine. If I hadn't laughed that same laugh for years, I might've been fooled by it, but I knew better. "I just about knocked myself plumb out!"

"I'd hate to see the door that does that to a person," was all I could find to say. My mind was racing a hundred and ten miles an hour. It felt like the room was turning upside down. I guess I'd been sitting pretty high up on that horse, and the trip down wasn't pleasant.

She took a drink of her milk and shook her head, her smile starting to fade.

"How much is a cheeseburger?" she asked to change the subject. I realized I'd never asked her if she wanted to see a menu—talk about a lack of manners—but in my defense, that shiny pink material stretched near to bursting over her belly had distracted me.

"Two dollars and forty-nine cents," I replied and got her a menu, taking a couple of deep breaths to calm myself.

"Oh, thank you, but I bet I won't be able to eat one after this big glass of milk and all these onion rings."

We both looked down to her empty plate. She'd cleaned her plate faster than anyone in Clayton's crew ever had, there wasn't a crumb on it. The poor kid must've been starving.

"I'll just have to get one next time."

"Would you like another glass of milk?"

She shook her head, but I got her one anyway. I noticed Pat was back at his spot in front of the deep fryers listening in on our conversation. But if he had something to say, he kept it to himself.

"Refills are free," I told her as I set the fresh mug in front of her.

She looked back down at the counter and I realized what I'd taken for lack of respect was plain old-fashioned shame. Pure and simple.

"My name is Millie." I held out my hand and she took it, her grip surprisingly strong.

"I'm Tipsy—I mean, my name is Tipsy. Nice to meet you."

"What kind of name is Tipsy?" I asked before I had time to stop myself.

"One that usually needs to be repeated a couple of times before people believe it's my real name. My mama— she's a real cut-up."

"Where is your mama?" I wondered what kind of woman would put a name like that on a baby girl.

"She's around somewhere. Last time I talked to her she was over in Friendship, but she wasn't there when I called this morning. I thought she might've come here, she said something about a job at the Bi-Rite down the road, she's a real good cashier—a people's person, you know? But I finally got ahold of her boyfriend and he said she'd gone down to Mobile with one of his buddies for a week or two."

So—I almost said out loud—that's the kind of woman that would name her baby daughter Tipsy. A *real* "people's person" from the sound of it. Boy had I pegged her wrong. While Tipsy stopped to take a big gulp of milk, I realized just how much we had in common. She had a lot to get off her chest and it sounded like she hadn't had anybody to listen. Nobody probably ever cared enough to ask her how she felt about anything. Well, anybody that knows me knows I don't mind asking a question or two.

"Do you have any other family?" I knew I was being nosy but now I was downright curious. Who was taking care of this child? And who was going to take care of the one that would be here in a couple of months or sooner? I had a lot of questions and she didn't seem to mind my asking.

"I have a sister," she nodded, "She's two years older than me. But she left last week to go to California.

"Why didn't you go with her?" She looked up at me and I noticed that one eye was green and the other one was blue. I hadn't noticed much about them until then except for the bruises.

117

"We ..." she patted her stomach, "wasn't invited."

"Honey, she just up and left you?" I couldn't even try to hide the sorrow in my voice.

"Well, I wasn't feeling up to traveling anyway, and I'm not really sure I want to go... She left me a box of her clothes, though, seeing how none of mine would fit me anymore. And she said she would try to save up enough money to send us a bus ticket once she got settled. She thinks she'll be the new headliner in a month or two, she is pretty flexible—they called her Bendy Wendy at The Boo..., uh, I mean The Bungalow where she used to work." Tipsy's face turned bright pink. She tried to change the subject but didn't do a very good job.

"Wendy used to take gymnastics..."

She reached down, self-consciously tugging at the hem of her dress, and I got the feeling she was trying to shut up. Well, I wasn't the brightest crayon in the box, but I knew by the look in her eyes not to push that subject any further. I helped her out and changed the subject away from her bendy sister who used to work at the Booby Bungalow. I knew all about place. It used to be Raylen's home away from home.

"What about your daddy?"

She shrugged right as the bell hanging over the front door chimed letting me know I had another customer. I'd never been so happy to hear that bell in my life. I needed a minute or two to collect my thoughts. I was flat-out perplexed. I'd never been so wrong about a person before— if you don't count Raylen—and I was conflicted. I didn't want anyone here to misjudge her like I had. Suddenly I felt very protective of Tipsy.

"Good afternoon, Bobby," I said a little too loud to the man in faded overalls causing him to jump. He recovered and made his way up to his regular place at the counter, nodding as he passed. Bobby wasn't much of a talker. "The usual?"

I put in an order for a cheeseburger and a bowl of vegetable soup before taking a mug out of the freezer. Bobby's been coming here every Tuesday and Thursday for years. He always orders a grilled cheese sandwich, a bowl of soup, and two cold Budweisers which he'd eat and drink while he read the paper. I poured his beer, watching the ice float up to the top of the glass while I thought of how to ask Tipsy the next question. Hell, I ain't never tiptoed around no one before, I figured now wasn't the day to start. I put Bobby's beer down in front of him and looked at Tipsy.

"What about your, um, the ... er," I didn't know what to call the fella that was partly responsible for her predicament, so I gave up and pointed towards her belly.

"Oh, he's ... well, he wasn't who I thought he was."

She touched her right eye gingerly and sighed. "My baby deserves better than that."

"And so do you."

I felt another flutter in my chest, but this felt like something coming loose instead of tightening up. Maybe this is what they mean when they say something tugs at your heart strings. Whatever it was, it was powerful.

"How old are you?" She was young, but she had more sense than me after I'd been married to Raylen for years. It took me a long time to realize that I had a choice in what I deserved.

"Sixteen," Tipsy sighed, lowering her voice to almost a whisper, "in two months."

"Where are you staying?" I asked straight out. The pitiful thing wasn't even old enough to have a driver's license.

"I have a friend who is letting me stay in her room until her parents get back from vacation. It's real nice."

"Where's your friend staying?"

"At her boyfriend's apartment." I rolled my eyes but kept my mouth shut and Tipsy giggled.

"I know, right? She has the nicest house—her room has that white and gold furniture that I always wanted, and her bed has lace hanging over it like a princess's or someone fancy, but she hates it and says it's a baby's room."

We both looked down at her belly.

"If only my baby could be so lucky." She patted him or her and smiled at me.

"What are you going to do when they come home?"

"Order up!" Pat shouted through the window, so I didn't get to hear an answer, if there even was one. I picked up the order and took a deep breath.

"Dangit! Pat's getting senile. I'll be right back with your sandwich, Bobby."

I put his soup in front of him and was surprised by the grin on his usually surly face. Bobby might not be much of a talker, but he was paying attention. I walked the cheeseburger back to the window.

"Pat, I need a grilled cheese," I said, and held up the burger, giving him a wink and a nod.

"It says right …"

"You need to get your glasses checked. Since when does Bobby eat cheeseburgers?"

I stared him down since the wink hadn't worked and he knew better than to argue. Instead, he lit a Camel right in front of the window, knowing dang good and well that nobody was supposed to smoke inside. I let it go. After all, I owed him one for the stunt I'd just pulled. Pat doesn't make mistakes in the kitchen. Ever.

"Here, Tipsy, I know you're not hungry, but it'll go in

the trash if you don't eat it and that'd be a shame. Pat makes the best burger in the state of Tennessee."

I glanced over my shoulder at Pat to see if he heard the compliment. He must have—he answered with a smoke ring in my direction.

"Thanks," Tipsy answered quick, grabbing the burger up before I had time to set the plate all the way down on the counter, completely forgetting to act like she wasn't hungry.

I picked up the pitcher of sweet tea and walked over to table four. My mind racing as I refilled Georgia and Shelby Jean's red plastic drinking glasses. Had Tipsy seen a doctor? Was she planning on keeping her child? Even if she wanted to, how could she? Was she in school? Did she want to be if she wasn't? Did her selfish, ignorant mama even know that her baby girl was pregnant? Would she care? Would she want to know that Tipsy was sitting here at my counter half- starved and beaten black and blue?

"Hey Millie," I heard a shriek and snapped back to reality. Looking down, I saw that the syrupy, sweet goodness that was known as Millie's Sugar Tea was a hair away from pouring over the rim of the glass into Shelby Jean's Frito chili pie.

"Sorry, Shelby Jean, I was pondering on something." I patted her shoulder and handed her a straw from the front pocket of my apron. "Use this until you drink it down an inch or two."

"She giving you trouble?" Georgia whispered, cutting her eyes over towards Tipsy.

I followed her stare and realized Georgia was seeing Tipsy the same why I had when she first came through the door. Georgia saw a piece of white trash in a tacky, tight dress looking for trouble. Every parent's worst nightmare, an unwed, pregnant teenager. She saw our hard-earned tax money flushed down the drain. A little hussy in the making, no doubt—probably somebody thinking that the world owed her something. But we couldn't have been more wrong.

What I saw now was a lost, little girl. A child lost to her own mama's ignorance and irresponsibility, paying for the stupidity of others. Someone who just wanted to be loved like everyone else, but who went looking for it in the wrong place. I saw me thirty years earlier standing with Raylen in front of the justice of the peace.

"Trouble? Lord, no. That's Tipsy. She might start working here some, helping Pat in the kitchen and giving me a break every once in a while." I listened as the words came out of my mouth, surprised as everyone else at the sound of them.

"Oh Millie ..." Shelby Jean piped in, shaking her head.

"Oh Millie what?" But I knew what was coming. I'd heard the same thing when I gave Pat a job years ago, back when he couldn't put the bottle down. He was living out of his truck after losing his trailer in a poker game and wouldn't nobody give him a break. But look how that turned out. He was the best cook in town. Not to mention he was a fine carpenter and mechanic. His skills kept this place running. No doubt about it, Pat was a damn good man. Close to fifteen years sober—which was all his own doing—and he never missed a day of work.

"Raylen always said you was too tender-hearted."

I took a deep breath and tried to make myself walk back to the counter and not hear her, but my feet weren't cooperating, and neither were my ears.

Georgia declared, "What was it he used to say to you? Oh, yeah, 'Quit picking up puppies off the side of the road.'"

They both sighed and shook their heads at me as I felt my ears burn hot enough to set my hair on fire. It took every ounce of will power not to douse Georgia's new updo with my sugar tea.

"Well, Raylen ain't here, is he? I pay the utilities here, don't I?" Always have. "And if I want to hire extra help, it's my business—Raylen can go to hell." I stopped right there and felt my shoulders relax. Then I aimed my grin at both those biddies, "Oh wait, he's already there."

Georgia and Shelby Jean gasped at the same time, sucking in so much air I felt the pressure drop in the room.

See, my husband, Raylen, died a couple of years ago when his heart gave out. He was a real piece of work. He'd left my face like Tipsy's more times than I could remember. He was selfish and greedy and wouldn't go out of his way to help anybody outside of his circle of poker-playing, cigar-smoking, skirt-chasing friends. And that was only if he knew he was going to get paid back with interest.

Raylen had a way to make everybody think that he was the first one there to help and the last one to leave. But in all the years I'd been married to him, I never knew him to get his hands dirty from working. Not once. Nobody ever knew the real Raylen. He could charm the skin off a snake. Yep, Raylen was a sneaky one and could talk circles around anybody. Mind you, he didn't like to have conversations, he just liked to talk. Lord, he thought that the sun rose just to hear him crow. He'd get everything so twisted up you didn't know if you were coming or going, and he could talk you into anything. I ought to know, he'd talked me into marrying him the day I turned sixteen. Had my mama's signature on the marriage license before he even proposed to me.

Tipsy had turned around and was watching us, so I

knew she'd heard me. I hadn't even asked her if she was interested in working here or what her plans were. I was real bad to fix everybody's problems for them—except my own. It took a heart attack to do that—and years of living had taught me that not everyone wanted their problems fixed. But it still didn't stop me from trying.

I walked back over to my side of the counter and patted Tipsy's hand. She looked at me, straight at me, and I was hoping that she was seeing me for the first time, too. I broke her stare when I noticed Bobby was running on empty.

"Bobby, you ready for another?" I got a fresh mug out of the freezer, knowing the answer before I asked. He gave me a wink and took a bite out of his grilled cheese. I guess Pat wasn't too mad at me, seeing as he hadn't banged on the bell when Bobby's order was up.

I turned back to Tipsy as I filled the new mug with Budweiser. "I have an extra bedroom upstairs, rent free while you work here. It's nothing fancy, no lace-covered princess bed or nothing like that, but it's not bad. We open at five a.m. for breakfast, so you could make a pan of biscuits before school—"

Tipsy sat up straighter at the word school.

"—and you could help with the dinner crowd afterwards, if it suits you. Of course, when the baby comes, you'll need some time to recover and you'll have homework and stuff that will be top priority."

She scooted off the stool and followed me on the opposite side of the counter as I walked Bobby's beer down to him.

"Are you serious? Seriously, are you serious?" I glanced her way and saw that her hands were shaking.

"We'll have to find a sitter during school hours because it gets busy here, but he—or she—could stay with us here in the afternoons. My office is right there." I pointed towards a room to my right.

"We could put a crib and a playpen in there for now." I swallowed past a lump in my throat. Years ago I dreamt of that, but since I never was able to have any youngin's of my own I'd buried that dream so deep I'd forgotten it.

"But, but ..."

"Now I won't be able to pay you much over minimum wage"—then again, I wouldn't be asking her to do a lot. She'd have her hands full with a new baby and school— "but like I said, the room is free, and you'll get three meals a day. Pat's not too hard to work with and most of the regulars are nice and easy to please. The high school is within walking distance on nice days, but the bus stops there on the corner if you'd rather take it. What else? Oh, a doctor. Do you have a doctor, honey?"

She shook her head and looked away, so I kept right on

going.

"The health clinic is right around the block. Those nurses are a hoot and sharp as tacks, you'll love 'em and they'll love you—they're regulars here. We'll get you set up on Monday. Oh, some comfortable clothes. Well, aren't we in luck?" I remembered the sign hanging in the window, "Ms. Katy's consignment store is having their annual half off sale. We could go on a shopping spree this afternoon. I'll front you the money and you can pay me back on installments. Hmmmm, I cain't think of anything else. Can you start tomorrow?"

I knew I was being extra pushy, but I was scared she'd chicken out. Sometimes it's harder to accept kindness from people than it is to accept meanness. It all depends on what you're used to. Something I knew for a fact.

We'd walked back to the other end of the counter— her mirroring me—and now she was standing directly in front of me. A single tear ran down her cheek as she reached up and hugged my neck. I hugged her back and felt the weight the girl was carrying on her shoulders let up a little.

"But why? You don't even know me," she whispered almost as much to herself as to me. I took her by the shoulders and stepped back so she could see my face. Really see me.

"Oh honey, yes, I do."

Tippy-Toe

"This wedding was filled with more drama than one of those shows on the Lifetime channel the wife loved so much."

Tippy-toe was the magic word. Your "get out of jail free" card, I reckon is a better way to describe it. If that word was so much as whispered by the bridegroom at any point during the ceremony he would be snatched up and physically taken out of the church, no questions asked. He would then be relocated behind the wheel of a getaway car provided by the best man. The requirements of the getaway car were as follows: a full tank of gas, five hundred dollars cash, and a credit card with no less than a five-thousand-dollar open limit—also belonging to the best man—in the glove compartment. And last, but not least, a case of beer on ice in a cooler in the back seat. It wasn't really a secret, even though people whispered when they mentioned it. That kind of thing has a way of getting out. And since the bride's older brother was in the same fraternity as the bridegroom, I'm sure even she'd heard of Tippy-toe before. I'd heard it several times myself over the years, sitting in the back pew, a witness to at least a hundred weddings. I couldn't help but wonder if today would be the day I'd actually see it come into play. My wife, the organist, had her reservations about the whole thing herself. She was like me—I like to think that we're in tune with our surroundings, others might say we're just nosy. They might be right. But we both thought this wedding had disaster written all over it.

For starters, the bride's father was gloating about how much money the groom was worth. With every sip of his flask he got a little more obnoxious about it. He couldn't say his future son-in-law's name enough. I'll be danged, if you hadn't known better, you'd thought you were at a political convention instead of a wedding the way the bride's father stood on the front steps shaking everybody's hand while he dropped the groom's last name left and right.

The bride's mother was no better. I was on my way to see a man about a dog when I found sweet Maisey Burke held hostage by her in the hallway outside the ladies' room. She had a glint in her eye, or maybe it was the smear of bright pink lipstick across her front teeth that kept Maisey immobilized. Whichever it was, I knew dern good and well it wasn't the conversation because Maisey was not one for gossip.

"It would be a waste of time now, don't you think? I never was too keen on the idea of her being a lawyer anyway. That's a man's job. I think she should start having kids right away, don't you agree?" I'm sure she meant heirs. Poor Maisey was too polite to run away, but too honest to answer. I pretended to have a coughing fit to give Maisey a chance to escape before I hurried past to the men's room.

The bride's sister was no help at all. All she did was sigh and moan while she repeated how lucky her sister was to land such a handsome, rich man. Then there was the whispered rumor that the bride was pregnant. Started by the groom's mother, I'm sure. No, I'm positive. Her exact words had been, "There will be a DNA test. She is not the first little gold digger to try and trap my son. She's just the first one to get this far..."

To make matters worse, the bride's brother, Jeff, spilled his guts to Eloise, that's my wife, in the kitchen when she went in to get us some coffee. She said he was on the verge of tears and once he started talking he couldn't stop. My wife, God bless her, has the kind of face—maybe it's her big doe eyes—that makes everyone pour their heart out to her.

Jeff told Eloise that he'd introduced the two of them, his sister and the groom, only a month ago. Seems like the groom, Trent's his name, had seen her on the tennis courts on campus and was quite smitten. Jeff laughed at him and said there was no way his sister would have anything to do with him. She was a good girl, saving herself for marriage.

Eloise said Jeff burst into tears.

"I had no idea Trent would propose to her just to get what he wanted! Kendall is way smarter than this, but she won't listen to a word I say. She's determined to go through with it." Eloise said he'd hung on to her like a life preserver as he cried on her shoulder.

Right after my wife told me about her encounter with Jeff in the kitchen, I happened to overhear the maid of honor talking to the best man. Well, not exactly talking to him. More like screaming. She was having a meltdown in the parking lot behind the church. Having stepped out to smoke a cigarette, I thought I'd be the only one out there—I was wrong. There seemed to be some unresolved feelings between her and the groom, to put it nicely.

It's amazing the things that go on at weddings if you pay attention. Most of the time it's sweet, funny, good things. Sometimes embarrassing things, but most of them good-natured. Things that the wife and I would laugh about as we lay side by side in our big, old bed, remembering our own wedding day. But this one was a fiasco. This wedding was filled with more drama than one of those shows on the Lifetime channel the wife loves so much. It was doomed for sure. If everyone was talking like this on their wedding day, I could only imagine what the rest of their lives would be like. I couldn't help but wonder if I'd finally hear someone use the not-so-secret, secret word. I hoped that the bride was as shallow as the rest of them and could stand the embarrassment of being left at the altar if it were to happen.

I stubbed out my cigarette, walked back in the way I'd come out, and took my seat in the last pew. You're probably wondering what I'm doing here.

Well, Eloise, is the only organist under the age of eighty for miles around, so she's asked to play most weddings. I, as her personal chauffeur, have attended more of them than any other human being I know. Eloise quit driving after she had eye surgery, but she enjoys playing the weddings. And to be honest, I enjoy going to them with her.

Crazy, I know, but most of them make me feel proud to be a married man myself. Add that to the fact that we're both retired and don't get out much, I guess it makes a little more sense, doesn't it?

It was time. I caught my wife's eye and we each gave a small shake of our heads. Maybe we were just a couple of nosy, old coots.

The groom's party was standing at the front of the church. The groom was a very handsome young man, even though he was a little green around the gills. Tall, broad shoulders, a dazzling smile, and perfect teeth. I could smell money all the way from where I was sitting. The girls came down one by one in the usual fashion, followed by the traditional flower girl and ring bearer. I kept waiting for something to happen between the maid of honor and the groom, but he never looked at her even though she was staring him down. He was too busy looking at the other girls behind her. They were batting their eyelashes and giving him their best smiles. It looked to me like they were trying to compete for the bride's spot. Even though they had to know about the drama with the maid of honor the night before and were supposed to be her friends. Heck, even the bride's sister was making googly eyes at him. Poor, stupid, young girls. Too many people think that money is the answer to everything.

Finally, the bride. Her father seemed to be having trouble making it down the aisle. He looked a little wobbly—too many sips from his flask, no doubt. The bride stood straight with her chin held high and made it down the aisle in spite of him. I couldn't wait to see the face behind the white lace. What sort of woman would she be? I was hoping she would be as rotten as the groom—give him and his family a run for their money. But when her veil lifted, I was completely surprised.

She was an innocent by stander, I was sure of it. There wasn't a bit of makeup on her naturally beautiful face and she looked happy. I mean the kind of happy that comes from being a genuinely good person. A person of intent. She definitely did not fit in with the rest of the crowd at all. She smiled at the preacher and then turned to face her husband-to-be. The look in her eyes was so open, so childlike. He was looking at her with a smug look of satisfaction and it was so obvious to me. He was an asshole and she had no idea what she was getting into. He was going to break her heart. How could we stand by and let this happen? He was going to embarrass her and shame her here in front of everybody. I expected her brother to break out in tears at any moment, but he stood tall beside the groom, wearing a stoical expression. He seemed to have given up and I fought the urge to yell, "Do something son! Don't just stand there." But no sooner had I thought this than I heard the dreaded word:

"Tippy-toe!"

In a rush of taffeta and a collaborative gasp from the

pews, all hell broke loose.

Quick as a wink, I looked up to see people running down the aisle, headed my way. I jumped up and opened the double doors that led outside. All I could think about at that moment was, at least let it be quick and spare her that much. I got swept up in the crowd and found myself standing on the steps in front of the church.

Quicker than you could spit, the escapee was placed in the car waiting at the bottom of the stairs. A tall figure in a black suit shut the car door, closing it on the long train of lace in the process. He then smacked the top of the car and said, "Get the hell out of Dodge, sis!"

I put up my hands up and caught the bouquet that came flying in my direction from the driver's window. I watched the turquoise '65 Mustang speed away and the sight of the bridal gown sticking out from under the door, waving in the wind, was a beautiful sight.

"Well, I'll be damned," I said.

The maid of honor was standing on the step beside me with a look of disbelief on her face. I handed her the bouquet. At first she recoiled from the gift, but then her expression changed from surprise to one of determination. She snatched it from my hand and ran inside to find the groom.

I turned to the tall figure in the dark suit, who was,

in fact, the former bride-to-be's brother, Jeff. He was standing there with the biggest smile on his face I'd ever seen on anybody.

The runaway's brother grabbed my wife by the hand and threw his arm around my shoulders.

"I *knew* my little sister was smarter than that. She's a genius! Thanks to the best man, she's got a nice little wad of cash to spend on her," he used his fingers to add quotation marks, "vacation cruise, and a sweet ride to get her to the port. Now, how 'bout a glass of champagne—on my dad—to celebrate!"

Something More

*"Jewel knows the crows arrive soon, then
the buzzards will come to finish the job."*

Jewel slips out the back door, mindful of the squeak in the rusted spring overhead. Her bare feet dart over the well-worn path through the woods behind the house, missing sharp stones and sneaky roots by memory.

When she reaches the edge of the field that lies on the other side of the woods, she stops to pick handfuls of clover. Jewel pinches the delicate stems close to the ground between her thumbnail and pads of her fingers, choosing only ones that are tall enough for tying. She works fast, slowing only to scold the bees that buzz around her.

"You quit bein' selfish. You got a whole field here

and ten more down the road. You can share this little bit with me." Her voice so seldom used sounds strange to her ears.

She tucks the clover into the front of her cotton dress, folding the frayed hem over the green leaves and purple blossoms. The flowers appear even brighter in contrast to the faded and well-worn step-ins that peek out from underneath her threadbare dress.

When she's sure she's picked enough, she turns and runs back to the woods, looking over her shoulder to make sure no one is watching even though she knows no one's there. It's a habit that's hard to break, like chewing the inside of her cheek until it's raw or poking the crooked bump on her collarbone where the broken pieces fused together without the help of a sling.

Certain she's alone, she slips between the branches of the weeping willow at the bend in the creek. Safe behind the curtain of branches she relaxes.

Jewel places the clover on the spongy green carpet of moss beside the willow that hides her most treasured items in the hollow of its trunk. Tucked away are pieces of quartz she found on the path. One perfect, turquoise-colored claw from a crawdad she found in the creek, a collection of feathers. Two books from her granny's house and a teacup with pink and yellow roses painted around the rim. The teacup is the only piece from her granny's set she'd been able to save. The rest were shattered against the kitchen wall, innocent victims of her stepfather's temper.

She looks at the clover and takes time to observe how each tiny petal grows together to form the perfect blossom. Lost in the moment, she traces the lines of white running through the green leaves with the tip of a dirty finger and takes in the beauty of each one. She sees that the edge of her thumbnail is bright emerald green and it makes her happy.

"Maybe someday I'll turn into a clover field," she tells the willow, "but right now I got work to do."

Starting with a single stalk, she weaves three strands of clover the way her granny taught her two years ago, on her sixth birthday. Her granny used to bake teacakes and biscuits, fix cups of sweetened milk and coffee and serve it to her in the cup with roses on it. Her granny's house smelled like chicken and dumplings and lavender from the garden. If the girl tries hard, she can still remember.

"Little Jewel," her granny used to say to her, "you are more precious than any diamond or ruby." And Jewel believed her. She finishes weaving the clover together and puts the two strands over her head to let them hang around her neck. Soon they become covered by tangles of unkempt curls.

After making sure the treasures are still hidden away, she peeks through the willow's branches. Jewel tiptoes out and takes off once again, breathing in the smell of the sun. It's almost too sharp, too busy. Like the vinegar fumes that linger in the kitchen when it's time for making pickles. Her hiding place smells like shade. The smell of damp bark, moist dirt, and roly-poly bugs. Of stillness and safety.

* * *

Last night Jewel saw the doe on the edge of the big highway. She and her mama were coming back from the laundromat with a load of clothes in the seat between them. The basket filled the car with the smell of fresh washed cotton, masking the stink of mildew and cigarette burns in the old Pontiac's carpet. The girl climbed up on her knees to bury her face in the warm pile of towels, something she couldn't do once they were folded and put away. Jewel smiled at her mama, wanting to share that goodness with her, but her mama hadn't seen her. She'd been too busy focusing on driving, exhausted after working a double shift at the café.

The girl studied the circles under her mama's eyes and the grey that had snuck into her hair. Hair that used to shine like black satin when she wrapped it around her fingers before she got too big to sit in her mama's lap. She looked at the foot pressing on the gas pedal and saw the bandage trying to hide a blister on her heel. She noticed the narrow ankle and skinny leg that looked too fragile to hold the weight of everything her mama carried on her shoulders. Jewel stared at her mama's face then, willing her to look at her. To notice her, to see anything but the bleak road that lay ahead. But the eyes of the doe caught Jewel's attention and she couldn't bring herself to look at her mama's wearied eyes again.

* * *

She bolts across the ditch that takes her to the highway and stops when she nears the doe's body. It's easy to imagine that she sees the ribcage rise and fall, but Jewel knows the deer isn't sleeping.

"You're a pretty girl." she says as a mourning dove calls to her from a limb of an ancient oak tree. "See, even he thinks so."

She looks for the soft grey feathers of her favorite bird but turns her attention back to the mama deer when she can't find them.

Jewel slides her fingers from the tip of the deer's nose to right above the large, almond-shaped eye. She examines the fur and realizes that what appears to be solid grey from a distance is brown, white, black, and grey combined. She's filled with wonder. The solid white fur around the doe's eyes is so clean and pure that the girl is careful not to touch it.

Remembering why she came; she takes one long strand of clover and doubles it twice making a small circle of flowers. Carefully, she slides it over the tall narrow ears of the doe and settles it above the brow bone, creating a perfect crown.

Satisfied, she stands and takes a long look. Jewel knows the crows will arrive soon, then the buzzards will come to finish the job. But for now, the mama deer deserves something more. Jewel sees the sun coming up over the top of the hill and realizes her own mama will wake up shortly. She leans over one last time and touches a black hoof, amazed at how small it is. She examines the long graceful leg that once carried the doe across the fields. It's surprisingly thin and looks oddly familiar.

Jewel feels a lump form in her throat and wipes a tear from her cheek onto the front of her dress.

She turns and takes off running once again, passes the willow without a glance and keeps going. Jewel races up the path, through the woods, avoiding stickers and briars that grow at the border of the yard. She doesn't slow down until she reaches the warped and rusty screen door of her back porch.

Jewel steps into the bare kitchen, respectful of the sharp edge on a piece of linoleum that's torn and curled at the corner. She catches her breath and untangles the second strand of flowers from her hair. She doubles the strand and doubles it again, making another clover crown. She treads softly over the worn carpet in the living room, past the hole in the cheap paneled wall left from her stepfather's fist. Past the odor of his aftershave that still lingers in the bathroom even though he's been gone for weeks.

She fights the impulse to run the length of the hallway, aware of the narrow space that offers no place to hide. She counts to five to slow the beating of her heart and raises the crown to her face as she tiptoes to the doorway at the end hall. She breathes in the safe clean scent before she steps into her mama's bedroom. Dread fills Jewel's small body until she sees the ribcage rise and fall beneath the thin sheet.

Lined up in a perfect row on her mama's nightstand beside a half empty glass of sulfury tap water are the pills her stepfather used to eat like candy. He'd shake the orange colored bottle and laugh at the rattling sound they made—the only time she'd heard him laugh. And the only thing he left behind.

Jewel hears the echo of his voice—almost as loud as the smell of his cologne—telling her mama to swallow them all at once and end her miserable life. She can still see her mama struggling on the kitchen floor, penned under her stepfather's knees as he tried to force her mouth open. And she can still feel the dead weight of her granny's pistol as she held it steady, pointed at the back of her stepfather's head.

Jewel holds her breath as she picks up the pills and slips them into the pocket of her dress, counting as she lets them fall. Three less than the day before. Crossing her fingers Jewel makes a silent wish that this is the last of them. She'll put them with the others beside her granny's pistol in her hiding place behind the willow's branches. Buried deep under the moss where no one will ever find them.

She creeps closer to the edge of the bed and studies the way the early morning sun falls across the pillow, catching the silver threads in her mama's hair. She's amazed at how they sparkle in the sunlight and she fights the urge to touch them.

"You are more precious than diamonds or rubies." Jewel whispers, then gently places the crown of flowers on her mama's head, careful not to wake her.

Hattie

"I wanted to go back to believing werewolves and the Carr's Creek Critter were the most frightening things you might find out there..."

Everyone in town said Hattie was crazy as a loon. If you'd ever seen her walking down Old Distillery Road, you would've believed them. When she wasn't barefoot, she wore a pair of old army boots at least two sizes too big. They caused her to drag her feet and stumble like the town drunk over loose gravel and black-eyed susan roots as she made her way back and forth to town. Sometimes she talked to herself, but nobody who was considered a credible source had gotten close enough to hear what she was saying. She was an outcast, but not considered a threat to anybody.

My friends and I always looked the other way when we saw her, the way our parents told us to do—without question. We thought we were being respectful, I guess. It never crossed my mind to talk to her, not even to say hello.

Trevor's brother, Craig, swore Hattie walked up on him once when he was changing a flat tire on the old highway. He said she was singing some weird song. By the time he told the story twice, he said she was walking with her eyes closed and the song she was singing was a lullaby which was creepy and started a few rumors, but Craig was so full of crap nobody gave him much credit.

Since Hattie was older than me and my friends, we hadn't known her in school. If she ever went, which was another mystery since nobody's older siblings ever talked about having her in class. And since she didn't go to church there was never a chance to get to know her. She lived alone in a house way back off the road and kept to herself, forgotten by everyone it seemed until she was spotted walking in town. Her house sat so far back you couldn't even see it in winter when all the leaves fell off the trees. She used to live there with her daddy and brother. But her brother died in Vietnam at the age of nineteen, then her father committed suicide a few years later.

Her mama had left town when Hattie was just a little girl. I knew that for a fact, because I'd heard my parents talk about it over the years. If we passed Hattie on the way to lunch after church Mama, nine times out of ten, would sigh and ask under her breath, "What would make a mother leave her own children?" Daddy never had an answer. No one seemed to know anything about Hattie's mama other than she left. It was a scandal no one wanted to be associated with. Mamas didn't up and leave their children, especially in the small town I grew up in.

Old Mr. Sumner, Hattie's daddy, was another story. Everybody knew him. He was crazy—mean crazy. Some people made excuses for him, because his wife left him and his son died at such a young age, but no one liked him. My mama warned me, the same as every other mama warned their kids, to steer clear of him if I saw him in town. And she made me promise that I would never go near his property. She was as scared of him as everyone else even though she wouldn't admit it. I asked her once why people were afraid of Mr. Sumner, but she shushed me with a "do as I say" lecture without answering my question. I did my best to keep away from Mr. Sumner and not because mama told me too. I stayed away because he gave me the creeps.

If I saw him coming, I automatically went the other way. I didn't need anyone to tell me to. But there was one time two years before that summer when I didn't notice him until it was almost too late.

Buddy, my beagle, and I had been coming home from my friend's house one evening. It was still light out, but after dinnertime. Toby's mom had cooked my favorite—liver and onions. I knew I wasn't supposed to like it—I'm sure there's a law somewhere that states no person under the age of twenty-one should—but I loved it. Toby always asked me to dinner when she made it because I ate second helpings which meant that left less for him. And because Toby was my best friend, he returned the favor when my mama made cabbage rolls.

Anyway, me and Buddy were crossing Main Street. I was pushing my bike across the street instead of riding because I'd knocked my seat loose earlier that day jumping ditches. I was ten-years old and thought I was indestructible. Wild Willy was my nickname and I'd earned it more than once. Toby, Jimbo, and Trevor had dared me to jump across the big culvert at the end of Carr's Creek knowing it was impossible and knowing I wouldn't turn down a dare. I bailed in mid-flight over the culvert and was able to land on my feet, but my bike smashed into the rocky bank. My seat took the hit, and it got twisted, loosening the bolt.

Like I said, I didn't see Mr. Sumner until he was right up on me in his old Ford truck. I'd looked both ways before crossing the street, my belly full of the rich dinner I'd just eaten causing me to walk slower than usual. I thought the coast was clear, but then I heard the roar of an engine and saw the grille barreling down on us from out of nowhere. Without a thinking twice, I grabbed Buddy's collar and dropped my beloved bike. It was one or the other. My bike was my pride and joy, but Buddy was my best friend.

Buddy yelped in surprise when I grabbed his collar. He tried to wrestle away from me, but I wrapped my arms around him and picked him up. I held him tight to my chest as he scratched and twisted, unaware of the danger we were in. I got us to the curb with Mr. Sumner's big blue Ford less than twenty feet behind us and coming up fast.

Once I made it to the curb, things seemed to go in slow motion, like I was watching a movie or something. I could see Mr. Sumner's hateful face through the windshield. He yelled and cussed at someone in the passenger's seat, yellow teeth bared as if he wanted to bite. His fist, a square weapon of knotty knuckles the shape of a brick, raised and shook like he meant to use it. I watched the spit as it sprayed out of his mouth, each droplet suspended in the air like some kind of magic trick. And I knew it was impossible, but I swear I smelled his rancid breath. It smelled of stale cigarettes, cheap whiskey, and potted meat.

He never took his foot off the gas. Not even when he saw me standing on the curb, his face inches from mine as he passed. He seemed unconcerned that he was driving on the wrong side of the street. When he ran over my bike lying in the middle of the pavement, he turned his head to follow me as he went by. He never once looked to see what he'd run over. Stared straight at me through the open window, his eyes—an unnatural shade of electric blue— filled with hate. As terrifying as that was, it was nothing compared to the way I felt when I searched the passenger seat.

I had one second to see who he was yelling at as he passed. My stomach dropped when I saw the seat was empty. There was no one there. No one I could see, anyway.

I waited until I could no longer see the tailgate of Mr. Sumner's truck, then I put Buddy down and we ran the rest of the way home. I was worked up pretty good by the time I got up the steps of our front porch. I felt those crazy eyes on me and heard his truck chasing us, even though I knew he wasn't there. I didn't feel safe until we were in the house with the door shut and locked behind us.

Mama rushed to me and started asking questions, but I

was bawling at that point and couldn't answer. She called for my daddy to come down from upstairs and together they checked Buddy and me for injuries. When she was certain that I wasn't bleeding, and no bones were broken, she got a cold washcloth for my face and a bowl of water for Buddy. I told her and my daddy what happened between sobs. I saw the look in my mama's eyes when my daddy said he'd go have a word with Mr. Sumner. She didn't say anything out loud, but her eyes said plenty.

No one had words with Mr. Sumner.

I finally calmed down and Mama fixed me a glass of warm milk. I ate homemade chocolate chip cookies at the dining room table while she sat close and stroked my shoulders. After I changed into my pajamas, she tucked me into bed. Something she hadn't done in years, and I didn't complain, I didn't even scoff when she left the hall light on. I was sure I'd have nightmares about being run over—or worse, kidnapped—by Mr. Sumner but I slept like a baby. Safe in the knowledge that my parents wouldn't let anything bad happen to me or Buddy.

Daddy never went to Mr. Sumner's house. Instead, he walked down the street and dragged my poor mangled bike home while I was inside, being babied by Mama.

The next day there was a new bicycle waiting in the drive for me. And not just any bike—the bright red Schwinn

Mark IV Jaguar, complete with a chrome headlight and stainless-steel fenders. The bike I'd been infatuated over for months. I was so excited about my new bike, I forgot all about the old one. We never talked about the incident with Mr. Sumner again.

When Mr. Sumner hung himself from a rafter in his barn a year later, there was a lot of grown-up talk concerning him. You know, the kind of talk that would stop when kids walked in a room. Lots of big words, like "inappropriate behavior," "psychosis," and "incestuous." Words that caused you to be uncomfortable, but you weren't sure why. No one ever took the time to talk to us kids about it. It was too awkward, too embarrassing, and maybe too much for the adults to admit that he was one of our neighbors.

Those kinds of people didn't fit into the perfect little world we lived in—with the block parties and cake walks, church socials and school bazaars. I guess it was easier for them to ignore the situation. Even though the adults quit talking about him after a while, we didn't forget him. His memory turned into something of a legend for us.

The summer I turned twelve, I was double dog dared to go to old man Sumner's house. Although I had promised to never go near his property, it technically wasn't his property anymore since he was dead; so I didn't really think I was breaking any promises to my mama. The only thing Mama had ever said to me regarding Hattie, was to leave her be if I saw her walking on the side of the road. Which I'd always done. I justified going to the Sumner's place by telling myself that Mr. Sumner no longer lived there. It didn't occur to me that Hattie did. Years of ignoring Hattie had made her invisible.

To tell the truth, Mr. Sumer had become even more scarier after his death. As crazy and mean as he was when he was alive, stories of his ghost were even worse.

I was twelve years old with an overactive imagination and still believed in haints and such. Story had it you could hear his ghost prowling around the woods near his house at night. Some people said they could hear him singing strange songs in a weird, high-pitched voice. People said the ghost of Mr. Summer was looking for money, long ago buried in mason jars, around those woods.

Mr. Avery saw the evidence himself when he was squirrel hunting with his dogs. He'd seen the holes dug out there in weird zigzag patterns around the pine trees. The fresh dirt piled around the holes, some as high as his knees. Of course, people teased him saying it was just holes left from squirrels looking for their winter stash, but he didn't believe it. He said his dogs wouldn't go near them and they were too big to have been left by any rodent. It spooked him so bad he refused to go back.

I know the truth now, and believe me, the truth is scarier than any ghost story I could ever make up. That summer I learned a hard lesson. I learned that people can be heartless, that monsters are real, and that sometimes they—the monsters—are living in your hometown.

Of course it was a full moon that night. The night I was double dog dared to go to Mr. Sumner's house, so I believed there was also the risk of running into a werewolf out there off of Old Distillery Road. We were spending the night with Toby. One of our favorite things to do in the summer. The four of us, Toby, Jimbo, Trevor and I, were camping out in his backyard in his dad's old tent. Each year we crept farther from the house, farther away from our parents and their rules. We built fires and cooked hotdogs and potatoes wrapped in foil, turned our marshmallows into flaming weapons and did all kinds of stupid stuff. We felt invincible, like most twelve-year old kids, and thought we knew everything.

Someone would steal a few cigarettes, and if we were lucky, we'd get our hands on cigars. Cigars were better because they lasted longer since you didn't inhale them—which we learned the hard way—and we felt older chewing on a lit cigar. We could actually feel the hairs on our chest sprouting and nonexistent muscles forming on our scrawny limbs with a soggy Dutch Master between our teeth.

It was getting close to midnight when the dare took place. We'd eaten everything, including the last marshmallow—Buddy saw to that—and were waiting for the light in the upstairs bedroom to go out. We couldn't light up our smokes until we knew the adults were in bed. No way we'd take the chance of Toby's mama catching us smoking—she was ruthless. Lord, if she caught us, it'd only be a matter of minutes until the volunteer fire department came roaring in. With sirens screaming and the hoses out to hose us down and humiliate us forever.

My mama would've never forgiven me.

We told stories to pass the time. We went through the usual, starting with the ghost of the old pilgrim walking down New Chapel Road. I'd seen her myself, cross my heart and hope to die. A couple of years ago, my brother was giving me a ride to Jimbo's. It was pitch black outside since the moon was hidden behind the clouds and there were no streetlights. She was walking down the side of the road dressed in a long, black dress, white apron, and bonnet. The headlights hit her, and she glowed. It seemed like the light reflected off her and you could see every detail crisp and clear. Shiny blond hair peeking out from underneath her bonnet, her eyelashes. Her hands folded together at her waist and the soft folds of her apron. Her bare feet, as white as milk, that didn't quite touch the gravel underneath them. It scared my brother so bad he wouldn't talk about it for months. Not a word until after he moved up to Knoxville to go to school and even then you had to beg him to tell the story. Not me. I couldn't shut up when it came to the pilgrim lady. I talked about her every chance I got.

Then there was the Carr's Creek Critter. I'd never seen it for myself, but it was described as some kind of Sasquatch type creature. Several of my friends' older brothers claimed to have had run-ins with it. Craig, who is so full of crap, said it looked more like an orangutan than Bigfoot and lives in the trees along the creek. Once I asked Mama if she believed the stories my friend's brothers told about the Critter. She laughed and said they'd probably had a run-in with a quart jar first and the rest was just their overactive, drunken, imaginations. She believed in haints, but not Bigfoot. Even though the first stories of the Critter were older than she was.

The stories seemed to take a natural shift from Carr's Creek to the old Sumner place. The widest part of the creek ran right past the Sumner house. Toby wanted to see if we could catch a glimpse of old man Sumner's ghost. It was the perfect night to go looking, the moon was so big and bright, it lit up everything. And we had a sugar buzz from the marshmallows to fuel us so of course, we all acted like it was a great idea. Nobody made a move, but everybody talked it up. I was a little slow on my comments, still thinking about the ghost of the pilgrim lady, so as luck—or lack of—would have it, I was the last voice heard.

"So, Wild Willy, you think it's a good idea?" Toby singled me out.

"Uhm… yeah, sure. Don't you guys?" I knew I wasn't very convincing. I scratched Buddy's neck and tried to act like I didn't know what was about to happen. Somehow, I'd been trapped. I figured it was payback for having talked Toby into sneaking an extra cigar from his daddy's cigar box. My daddy smoked Lucky Strikes.

"What, are you scared?" Jimbo piped in, grinning like a shit-eating dog.

"No. Are you?" I shot back.

"You're not scared?" Toby and Trevor both said at the same time.

"Nah, I'm not scared. Are you scared?"

That was the best I could do. I knew I was done for. I was too busy trying to think of a way to get out of what I knew was coming next to come up with something better.

"Ha! If you're not scared, why don't you go?"

"I thought we all were…" shit, "weren't we?"

"I dare you to go and knock on the front door." Toby was looking straight at me.

"Knock on the door? Why? You think Mr. Sumner's ghost is going to invite me in for cookies and milk?" I laughed my best tough guy laugh, but it came out a little higher pitched than I'd meant it to. We went back and forth for several minutes.

Then Toby said the dreaded words and there was no turning back.

"I double-dog dare you to knock on Sumner's door." That was all it took. I'd never backed down from a double-dog dare. We headed out, Buddy at my side.

To get to the Sumner's house from Toby's, you had to walk through the woods and follow Carr's Creek for about a mile. They were going to stay with me until we saw the house, then hang back and watch to make sure I made it up on the porch to the door. It was easy going at first. We followed the well-worn path we'd made years ago to a swimming hole at the bend of the creek, then climbed over an old cedar tree that marked the end of Toby's property. We'd never gone past the cedar until that night. I didn't know if anyone else felt it, but the air seemed to change once we crossed the invisible line that separated Toby's place from the rest of the woods. It felt colder and kind of heavy on the other side of the cedar.

The moon shined its white light down on the woods like a beacon, so bright you could see everything clear. Like a spotlight was following us and lighting up the entire forest. On one hand I was glad for the light, but sort of wished we weren't so visible to werewolves or polecats or possibly the "critter." The moon reflected off the creek and everything seemed eerily peaceful. Until ...

I was the one to see her first, but I assumed she was some kind of animal digging in the dirt. Once my eyes focused, I realized that whatever was there was too big to be a squirrel or a racoon. I stopped and held up my hand to the others.

"Hey," I whispered, "I think it's the critter." Toby heard me and stopped, but Jimbo and Trevor weren't paying attention and ran into us pushing us closer. Our heels slid in the damp leaves as we struggled to stay upright.

"What'ja stop for?" Jimbo asked, completely oblivious to the fact that Toby and I were pushing against him. Toby shushed him and pointed.

"What the hell?" Trevor asked, already turning to run.

"That ain't the critter, that's old man Sumner's ghost." I whispered as my eyes adjusted to the shadow just past the moonlight's reach and I could see that the thing in front of us had a human shape. Then we heard a voice.

"Rock-a-bye baby, in the treetop,

When the wind blows, the cradle will rock,

When the bough breaks, the

cradle will fall."

Jimbo and Trevor turned on their heels and ran like little sissies right back the way they'd come. They never looked back. Toby and I figured out in the same instant that it wasn't a ghost after all. It was Hattie.

"Do you think she's the one digging for the old man's money?" Toby whispered in my ear.

Before I could answer, Hattie looked up. Toby grabbed my arm and squeezed it hard enough to leave a bruise, but I didn't pull away. She was looking right at me and the last of the lullaby seemed to fall from her mouth. "… and down will come baby, cradle and all."

She stood up slowly, never taking her eyes off me.

"Oh, shit!" Toby yelled and let go of my arm. He turned and ran like hell, following Jimbo and Trevor back to the safety of the campfire.

I'm not going to lie, I would've run too, but Buddy took off in the opposite direction; straight towards the Sumner house. I couldn't leave without my dog. I tried to call him, but I couldn't make a sound. My heart was thumping against my ribcage so hard, I thought it was going to bust through. When I opened my mouth to call Buddy's name, nothing happened.

"Do you know where he is?" Hattie held her hand out to me. I stood there trying to understand what was happening. Where who is? Mr. Sumner? Buddy? I couldn't have answered her even if I knew what she was asking.

"Do you know where my baby is?"

I swallowed hard and felt my knees turn to jelly. I had to focus to stay upright. Hattie was looking at me, but I don't think she was seeing me. She looked like she was sleeping with her eyes open. I couldn't do anything at that point but stand there, frozen on the spot and hope that Buddy would come back to me on his own. As soon as he did, we'd hightail it back to Toby's.

She kept on talking. "I used to hear him cryin', but I cain't hear him no more. He was such a tiny little thing. Daddy took him away and I never saw him again. I never even got to feed him. I know he's hungry."

That did it, I snapped out of whatever kind of trance she had on me and yelled, "Buddy! Come on now!"

My voice had the same effect on Hattie as hers did on me and she appeared to wake up from her daze. She straightened her dress, wiped her hands clean on the folds of her skirt, and pulled her hair away from her face. She cleared her throat and said, "Buddy? Buddy's in the barn where he always goes."

My blood turned to ice and I almost ran. I hate to admit it, but I almost left my dog behind. How in the blazes did she know my dog? Why would Buddy be in the barn? Old man Sumner hanged himself in that barn. "What are you doing out here?" she asked, sounding suddenly normal, which scared me almost as much as when she was talking crazy.

I stuttered, scared shitless, but then I heard myself say, "We were looking for the Carr's Creek Critter. I don't think we meant to come this far ... and then my dog, he run off."

Once I started talking I was so nervous I couldn't keep my mouth shut. I was rambling and asked before I could stop myself, "What are you doing out here so late?"

"Looking for my ... looking for something I lost a long time ago." She rubbed her hands on her dress again and turned to look over her shoulder.

She peered into the dark shadows in the thicker part of the woods and then turned back to me.

"This tree here fell on top of something last night and I cain't get it off."

I saw Hattie had been trying to move a big limb that had fallen, not digging in the dirt like I'd first thought.

"Would you help me?" she asked.

"Um ..." I saw Buddy running a few yards away. I

yelled for him again and he came towards me before turning around and taking back off again. I wanted to chase after him and yank a knot in his tail for ignoring me, but I did not want to go closer to the barn.

"Would you help me move that limb?" Hattie asked again, taking a step closer.

When I turned around, we were less than five feet apart. It was the first time I'd ever really looked at her and I was surprised at what I saw. Hattie was pretty. I mean, she was really pretty, prettier than any other girl I'd ever seen in person.

The moonlight shined down on her while I stood there staring. Her eyes were the same bright blue as her daddy's had been the day he almost ran me over, but they didn't seem to have any meanness in them. There wasn't a crazy, wild look in them either—they looked sad, but kind of hopeful. Her teeth weren't spikes or fangs, and her hands weren't claws. They were small and delicate, like my mama's but her nails were short and unpainted. And her hair wasn't dirty and tangled, like everyone always described it. It was clean—I could smell the scent of the same apple shampoo we used coming from her thick dark tresses. Hattie was just a girl, not a ghost or a monster. I suddenly felt foolish for being so afraid of her.

I didn't know what else to do but help her. I mean, I had two options—I wasn't going to chase Buddy around the barn, and I couldn't leave without him. If I stalled long enough, maybe he'd get tired of running around and come back to me. I forced my legs to move and walked over to investigate the limb. It appeared to have fallen across a flower bed.

"I think I can roll it down into the trees over there. Will that work?" I asked.

Hattie didn't answer. She was looking at some flowers pinned beneath the fallen limb. I tried to be careful and not step on them as I pushed with everything I had. It didn't budge. I found a smaller branch close by to use as leverage and finally got it moving. I was so caught up in what I was doing I didn't notice the big rock pressed into the ground under the weight of the fallen section of oak tree.

I stepped sideways and tripped over it, landing flat on my back on a cushion of leaves and moss.

When I sat up, Hattie was beside me on her knees, standing up the flat, rectangular shaped rock that caused me to fall. I realized the river rock was a makeshift headstone.

"Shi... is that a grave?" I asked, scooting backwards like a crab, my heels slipping across the damp leaves.

"Yeah, but don't be scared. There ain't nobody in it."

I had a fleeting thought that maybe I was the one sleepwalking and this was all just a bad dream.

But then I heard her voice asking, *"Do you know where he is?"* I jumped to my feet, no longer needing to pinch myself to see if I was awake.

Hattie straightened her back and focused her eyes on me. She rubbed her palms on her skirt and sighed. She stood, smiled and said, "Well, where are my manners? I ain't used to having visitors. Would you like some tea? I've got some sun-brewed sweet tea on the porch."

She turned towards her house and kept talking. "It's special. The secret is the mint I put in it. I learned that from my mama."

There was no way I was going to drink anything she gave me, and I wasn't going near her house. She might not be the monster everyone described, but she definitely wasn't normal. I ignored her and looked once at the blank tombstone and then up at the barn. I yelled, "Buddy! Get over here right now! BUDDY!"

That's when she laughed. An unsettling laugh that sounded more like the caw of a crow than the laugh of a girl. It made goosebumps pop up all over my body.

"Of course not." She said, "What was I thinkin'? You didn't come for a visit, it's near midnight. You was lookin' for monsters, right? Maybe you was thinkin' the

Critter was my fella? Hopin' you'd get a glimpse of us smoochin' on the porch swing I bet. Now that'd be a good story to tell. I don't reckon I've heard that one yet." I saw something change in her blue eyes and she looked years older. "I thought you was different, but you ain't no better than the rest of them."

She started walking in the direction of the barn. I stayed where I was and listened to her talking. "Boys come up here at night, yelling things too horrible to repeat. Telling me all the things they'd like to do to me, banging on my windows. Leaving trash in my woods, beer cans and cigarette butts all over the place. Calling me names..."

Hattie stopped and turned around. I thought she was mad, and I was expecting her to fly into me, but the look on her face was a sad one.

She shook her head and threw her hands in the air. "You just gonna stand there, or do you want to get your dog?"

I looked behind me, hoping to catch a glimpse of Toby but he wasn't there. I turned back to Hattie feeling like a rat in a trap. "Well come on then." She motioned for me with a flick of her hand, "I'll show you where Buddy likes to go."

I silently cussed Toby and Buddy's name both while I followed behind Hattie. How did she know anything about

Buddy or what he did? I stayed alert, ready to run if she tried to grab me or hit me over the head with something. Hattie started talking again.

"Sometimes I cain't sleep and wind up out in the woods. I guess I sleepwalk but it ain't like my cat can tell me whether I do or not. Do you ever sleepwalk?"

I didn't answer, I was too busy calling Buddy's name, but she didn't seem to care. I didn't think she was talking to me anyway. I had the feeling she talked to herself all the time.

"Sometimes I wake up down by the creek with no idea how or why I got there." She slowed her pace to wait for me catch up with her. I stopped a couple of feet behind and felt a shiver run up my spine, like someone walked on my grave. The thought of her prowling around the woods at night in her sleep was unnerving. I wondered how many nights the boys and I'd been sitting around the campfire in Toby's backyard, telling ghost stories, and roasting marshmallows while Hattie was right on the other side of the trees. Sleep walking and singing to herself. All alone, tending to an empty grave.

I was so afraid that my entire body felt like it hummed with an electric current. As soon as I got ahold of Buddy, we were running back to Toby's as fast as we could.

Hattie stopped in front of the barn door and once

again, I willed my knees to hold me up. Never in a million years had I imagined I'd get so close to Mr. Sumner's barn. But here I was without any witnesses that could testify on my account or a single dare to make me do it. I wondered how long it would take for my parents to find my body. I called Buddy one more time, hoping my stubborn dog would finally come to me so we could get the heck out of there.

Hattie jumped when I yelled Buddy's name that time. She turned and scowled, "Hush! Are you hard of hearin' or just hard-headed? I told you it won't do you no good to call him. Buddy won't come. You'll understand when you see."

She pushed the big door open and I felt my teeth chatter in my head like they did when I was freezing, even though I had sweat running down the center of my back. If she was going to kill me, I hoped she'd be quick about it. I didn't think I could put up a fight, my legs and arms were stiff as boards. I had one second to think at least I would die with my dog as Hattie reached up over her head. She grabbed a chain attached to an overhead light and pulled. I blinked against the glare and thought my mind was playing tricks on me.

A big loom sat in the center of the floor holding bright strips of material weaved through sturdy white cord. Stacks of material, sorted by color, lined up on one wall. On the far wall a finished rug hung over a rack. I don't know what I thought I would see. Blood on the walls, or the old man's body hanging from the rafter? Human bones? Not a colorful rag rug like the one at our house.

"Ain't what you were expectin' I guess." Hattie said as a grin stretched across her face. I could see she was having fun picking on me.

"We have a rug just like this one in our kitchen." I said, pointing at the finished rug on the rack. My voice came out a little higher pitched than normal, but I was so relieved to still be alive I wasn't embarrassed.

"I know. I give it to your mama as a thank you." Hattie scoffed, "She brings me most of the material I use for my rugs. She holds that clothes drive twice a year down at y'alls church and brings me the clothes that ain't fit to wear. Plus, she gathers up all these old sheets from the hospital that I dye different colors. They might be worn mostly through, but they make a good rug."

Hattie did a half turn and looked around her workspace. She leaned down to pick up a loose cord off the near spotless floor and dropped it in a trash bin. The barn was as clean as my daddy's garage and almost as organized as Mama's sewing room.

And here I thought I was walking into a slaughterhouse.

She looked at me and smiled, "That's how come I

know your dog. He used to come out with your mama. She's real nice and awful pretty, ain't she? Once she brought me a fancy cake from that bakery downtown, but she couldn't stay to have a piece with me—being so busy and all." Hattie's eyes drifted over to the corner. She shook her head and continued, "Buddy though, he found his way back for some cake and has been coming back to visit ever since. Look over there, there's your sweet pup."

She pointed to a wooden crate turned up on its side in one corner of the room. Snuggled up in a burrow of scrap material was Buddy, lying beside another dog. He stood up when he noticed me. He flattened his ears and tucked his tail between his legs knowing he was in trouble.

"Surprise." She giggled, "He's a daddy."

Dumbfounded, I saw there was a litter of pups beside the small wired-hair terrier that Buddy had been laying with. I looked at the pups and back at Hattie. She grinned and I watched as she walked over to the puppies and squatted down to scratch the mama dog behind the ears. Buddy, obviously familiar with Hattie, wagged his tail and leaned against her. I watched Buddy as he pushed his nose behind Hattie's ear, nuzzling her until she laughed and gave him a pleasant scratch down his back. I wondered how something so normal could happen in a place where nothing was close to normal.

"Yeah, your hound is smitten with little Nelle. I tried to chase him off at first, 'cause I knew y'all would miss him. But I think he only comes around when you're at school and he's so dang sweet. Plus, he's good company. Even to Tomcat. You should see them two, a beagle and a cat, layin' on the porch together. And of course, little Nellie Girl is crazy about him. I think she misses your old hound when he's not around."

Maybe standing in the bright light of the barn listening to Hattie talk about her pets. Or maybe learning that Buddy knew more about her than I did, gave me courage. I still don't know what made me do it, but I took a step closer to Hattie and asked, "Are you looking for a real... a live baby? Or did your baby die?" I swallowed hard and asked the next question. "Is that his grave?"

She rubbed her hands up and down her skirt and that's when I realized she was as scared as I was. She'd been doing that nervous thing with her hands in the woods. Hattie took a deep breath and answered without so much as blinking.

"Yes, I am lookin' for a real baby, but, no, he didn't die. I mean, he's dead by now—of course he is, but he was still alive when I saw him last. My daddy took him out in the woods somewhere right after he was born. The least I can do is find him and give him a real grave to rest in."

My stomach flipped and everything came together. I won't say it made sense, because there was nothing about it that made sense, but I thought I understood. Neither one of us spoke for a few minutes while Hattie busied herself with the puppies.

"Is that why your daddy killed himself? Because of what he done?"

"I done it."

I was confused. "You? Wait, I thought you said your daddy ..."

She spun around; her blue eyes bright as a flame. "He didn't kill himself. I done it." Hattie made a fist with her right hand and jabbed her thumb in the center of her chest. She didn't look nervous anymore, or strange. She looked determined.

"I killed him. He was goin' to put me up in the loft to keep me from tellin' anybody about what he'd done. He drug me up there with a rope to tie me up with, like I was a stray dog. But once we got up there, he started doin' other things. The things he's done to me since mama left."

Her fist uncoiled and she put both hands flat on her chest. "I couldn't let him put another baby in me to take out in them woods to leave for raccoons or coyote to drag off. He'd already strung up the rope on the rafter and had a loop in the other end to tie my hands together. When he let go of me to unbuckle his belt, I kicked him in the stomach as hard as I could."

I let out a breath I hadn't known I was holding as Hattie took in a deep one. She tucked her hair behind her ear with a shaky hand. Red splotches had sprung up on her cheeks and neck that looked like they'd burn you if you touched them.

"When he fell down a hollerin' and cussin', holdin' hisself, I put the end of the rope he was intendin' to tie me up with over his head and slid him over the edge of the loft like he wasn't nothin' but a bale of hay."

She paused and we both looked up towards the upper floor. Hattie shuddered, and I saw something pass behind her eyes. "He was dead as a doornail by the time I come down out of the loft."

Hattie went back to the puppies and picked one up that was rooting in a corner. I saw that it had markings just like Buddy. She kissed the top of the puppy's head and gently ran her thumb down the its muzzle before she placed it closer to its mama. "I don't think he ever knowed what happened. I ain't never fought him before. But after what he did, I wasn't fightin' for myself. I couldn't let him do what he did to another little baby. He thought I was his to do with whatever he wanted, but that baby was mine. I was supposed to protect him and I didn't."

175

She turned back to me and we stood there looking at each other as I struggled with a bunch of emotions at once. Disgust, shame, sadness and fear fighting for first place. Hattie looked relieved to have told her story, which made sadness take the lead.

"Have you ever told anybody else about what happened?"

Hattie stared at me so long before she answered, I didn't think she was going to. But then she blinked and turned away.

"Ain't nobody asked ever asked." She shrugged and rubbed her hands a couple of times.

I let what she said sink in. I thought she was waiting for me to say something else, or ask another question, but I was speechless.

"Everybody thinks I'm crazy, but I ain't. Well, I might be crazy, but I ain't dumb." She looked at me and managed a smile, but I couldn't smile back.

We watched each other for a minute in silence, and I felt a wave of guilt run through me, erasing everything else I felt. All the things I'd heard about Hattie, I'd never tried to find out anything for myself. I'd listened to the stories and ignored her like everyone else.

Hattie sighed a sad sigh and suddenly looked ten years older, the red splotches still on her skin, but not as bright.

She turned away from me. "You better get home, it's late. Your mama'll be worried about you." She took a strip of material and tied it around Buddy's collar. She scratched his ears, kissed the top of his head, and handed the makeshift leash to me. "Just in case he thinks he's stayin'." I reached for her hand but changed my mind at the last minute and took her wrist instead. We did some kind of awkward handshake as I felt my cheeks start to redden. I had the urge to hug her, but it felt wrong. Too personal.

I didn't even know her.

Even after hearing her most personal secrets, I realized we were still strangers.

* * *

Buddy and I left Hattie there all alone with her terrible memories and empty house. We walked back through the woods towards Toby's place. I was too tired to run, and I didn't feel the need anymore. When we got to the cedar that marked Toby's property, I wanted to turn around and go back. Tell Hattie I was sorry. But I didn't know where to start, or exactly what I wanted to apologize for. I was sorry for everything she'd been through.

As I came up the last rise, I could see Jimbo, Trevor,

and Toby all sitting together around the fire. They were on the far side, their backs towards the house so they could keep an eye on the woods. Sitting as close as possible to each other without being on each other's laps. They jumped when we came into the clearing.

"Holy shit, what was that all about?" Toby shot up on one knee like a jack-in-the-box.

I sat down beside Trevor without answering and Buddy crawled into my lap.

"Shit-dogs, did that really just happen?" Trevor had the nerve to laugh.

"I can't believe y'all left us there. You bunch of sissies. You just run off." I scowled at them, feeling angry all of a sudden.

"Well, what the hell happened to you? I thought she'd drug you into the house or something." Jimbo said.

"And what if she had? What would you've done? I couldn't just leave Buddy, could I?" I gave them all a look that let them know I didn't want to talk about it. But no one paid attention.

"I can't believe we saw her out there." Jimbo said.

"What'd she say?" Toby asked and my friends all looked at me grinning. They wanted to hear something they could repeat tomorrow. A story that would get them some attention. I felt my anger rise up inside of me and let it loose.

"This ain't a ghost story anymore. All that bullshit is just plain old gossip. Hattie is a person—a girl, living all by herself without a brother or mama or... anybody." A lump formed in my throat. "I don't want to turn what happened tonight into another tale to be told by everybody."

I saw the looks of surprise on my friend's faces. They'd been expecting a story, of course they had. This was the kind of thing we lived for. But I wasn't going to give it to them.

It wasn't my story to tell.

I tried to light a cigarette—I didn't even care if Toby's mama saw me—but my hands were shaking so bad I couldn't keep the match head on the striker. Toby struck a match for me and held it steady.

"Dang, Willy. I've got to tell my brother, he'll shit his pants!" Jimbo laughed, and I turned to him. His goofy grin made my stomach turn and I felt sick. I thought of Hattie saying that I was no better than the other boys who drank beer in her woods and yelled nasty things at her for fun. I'd never heard anyone talking about that before, but now I wondered if Jimbo's brother was one of them. If so, did Jimbo know about it? Would he think that was funny?

"Yeah, you want me to tell him you and Trevor took off running like little chicken shits? That you dang near peed your pants and didn't even come looking for me? Is that what you want everybody saying?" I leaned towards him to let him know I meant business. Then I looked each one of them in the eye.

"You want everybody to know ya'll left me there? Because I'll tell it."

"Okay, okay. Cool your jets, Willy. Shit." Toby said while Jimbo gawked at me. Thankfully Trevor stayed quiet.

"She's just a person, that's all." I said, scared I might cry if I said anything else. Part of me wanted to tell the story, to unload the weight of it, but I knew what would happen. It'd get turned into another tale and people would be even more afraid of her. Or worse, she could get into trouble. Maybe even sent to prison for murder. Either way it went, wouldn't anything good come of it for Hattie.

We sat there for a few minutes in silence. My hands were still shaking, and I was having trouble swallowing past the lump that formed behind my Adam's Apple. I knew they were confused by the way I was acting, but I didn't care. I could see Trevor out of the corner of my eye—raising his shoulders and eyebrows at Toby. Toby coughed and messed with the fire. Then Jimbo remembered he'd snuck a half-empty pint jar from his daddy's stash and went to get it out of his backpack.

"Here, Willy," he said offering the moonshine to me. I

took it and tossed back a hefty drink. I shuddered when the moonshine hit the back of my throat threatening to come back up, then took another when it didn't. I looked over to Toby and he stared at me.

"That was the scariest thing I've ever seen in my life." Toby said, and I agreed.

He didn't even know the half of it.

I handed him the jar and he passed it on to the others after taking a sip.

We watched the fire die out and finished off the moonshine. Jimbo and Trevor got into the same old argument about who had the best boobs—Marilyn Monroe or Brigitte Bardot. They usually made me laugh, but after everything I'd learned at Hattie's, I just didn't feel like laughing.

After a few minutes I went inside the tent and got in my sleeping bag. Buddy lay down at my feet and I realized the strip of material Hattie had tied to his collar was still attached. I untied the knot and stuck the soft fabric in my pocket, the thought of throwing it away felt wrong. It wasn't too long before the rest of the guys came into the tent and the moonshine put them right to sleep.

But no matter how hard I tried, I couldn't fall asleep.

Those foreign sounding words the adults used after they found Mr. Sumner's body kept whirling around in my head. Along with the definitions I'd looked up in the big dictionary in the school's library a long time ago. Words that had not made any sense back then, started to fit like pieces of some warped puzzle. If they'd known what was going on, why hadn't anybody done anything about it? My parents were good people. They went to church every Sunday. Mama cooked meals for our neighbors when they were under the weather and Daddy volunteered to do yardwork and run errands. And Toby's parents were good people, they were both volunteers at the fire station and his daddy was a deacon at the church—how could they ignore what was happening to Hattie all those years? Our preacher was a good person, always talking about how we should help each other and treat people the way we wanted to be treated. How could they all turn a blind eye? I kept hearing Hattie say that no one had ever asked her what happened.

Up close, Hattie hadn't looked that much older than me.

We got up right after sunrise and helped Toby take down the tent. Usually we'd sleep late, then hang out as long as possible. Take our time going home and put off chores as long as we could, but not that morning. Jimbo and Trevor took off together without one word about what had happened the night before.

Now that Jimbo and Trevor had left and after thinking about it all night, I wanted Toby to ask me what happened. But he didn't. I think he knew I wanted to tell him something but was afraid to hear what I might say. He shook his head and tried to laugh when I started to say something.

"Whew, she really is crazy, I reckon," Toby said, leaning down pretending to tie his shoelace. It was already tied in a tight double knot, so he busied himself straightening out is socks instead.

"I don't know. Is she crazy, or just—hell, I don't know?" I really didn't know. I mean she wasn't normal, but how could she be after everything that'd happened to her? Had she always been that way or was it what happened to her that made her that way? What had that mean old bastard done with her baby? Was it really his baby? Was that even possible?

I had a lot of questions and no clue what the answers where, or who to ask. I couldn't ask my mama; she would have had a conniption fit. She'd be upset that I'd gone out there on a dare. And I was pretty sure she wouldn't like me knowing she'd been out there before. If she didn't care, why hadn't she said so? Why hadn't she said, "Oh, look at this nice rug Hattie gave me?" Instead of acting like she'd bought it somewhere.

Why hadn't she asked for my help to take the clothes to Hattie? She asked for my help all the time when she took loads of clothes to church.

Was she ashamed of going there? Was she afraid that Hattie's kind of crazy was contagious? I think deep down, it was the fear that Mama would lie to me about going out to Hattie's that stopped me from asking. If Mama lied, I don't think I could ever look at her the same way. I'd have a whole other slew of questions and no one to ask.

No way I could ask my daddy. He wouldn't have a clue how to talk to me about something like that. When he tried to tell me about the birds and the bees last year it was so painful and awkward, I let him off the hook. I told him we had a class at school that explained it all and he was so relieved I thought he was going to do a backflip. And that was just a boring talk about how babies were made. I couldn't ask him about what Mr. Sumner forced his own daughter to do. Neither Mama or Daddy would think that was an appropriate conversation to have with a twelve-year-old boy. It was too ugly, too unpleasant. It didn't fit into our world. The safe, comfortable world we had built for ourselves. The nice world we lived in, in our pretty Victorian house on the square where home baked cookies and warm milk made everything okay.

In the end, I guess I wasn't much different. I did like everyone else had done in that little town. I didn't say anything about what happened to anybody. Believe it or not, my friends and I never talked about it again. If they told anybody else, I never heard about it.

After a month or two I finally threw away the strip of material Hattie tied to Buddy's collar. I buried it under a banana peel and some other trash in the bin and tried my best to forget the whole thing. I never went back to Hattie's, even though I thought about going back to see if there was anything she needed help with. Or to let her know I didn't blame her for what she did to her daddy. To tell her I was sorry for what happened to her. But I couldn't bring myself to go back, there was so much sadness and so many things I didn't understand. And to be perfectly honest, I was a coward. I didn't want to know anything else.

If I saw Hattie out walking, I would nod—if there was no one around—but she acted like she didn't know me. I hoped that life as I'd known it before I learned about Hattie's secrets would keep going along. And it did.

But I had a nightmare for years after that summer. Still do, sometimes.

Each time I wake up in a sweat unable to fall back

asleep for hours afterwards.

It's the same dream, over and over.

The one where I'm in the woods with Hattie and she's pleading with me to help her, she is *begging* me for help.

And I just walk away.

Fucking Hipsters

"Two more feet and they would've dug into Chief – just two fucking feet."

Frank Lewis sits in the hard, plastic chair across from the court-appointed therapist and avoids eye contact, choosing to stare at the box of tissues on the table between them. He can't bring himself to look into the soft, brown eyes behind the horn-rimmed glasses. The eyes remind him of his late wife. He wonders what Hazel would think if she could see him now. Frank isn't sure if she would be upset or proud of him for what he's done to wind up here. Mostly proud, he thinks, but either way it doesn't matter because Hazel is gone.

The therapist holds the patient's folder in her lap,

unopened. She didn't introduce herself and she hasn't spoken a word. She knows the nurse told Mr. Lewis her name, she'd been standing outside the door listening to the nurse talking nonstop without giving him a chance to answer even if he'd wanted to. She hopes that her silence will make a difference. And anyway, her name badge lets him know who she is, not to mention the white coat. Alice feels for the older patients who are spoken to like slow witted children and treated like they've lost their marbles. Often times she's thought that if she were in their position, she'd stay quiet too.

She knows what the initial diagnosis is regarding Mr. Lewis, but she isn't convinced that he suffers from dementia or a schizoaffective disorder. She doesn't think Mr. Lewis is crazy or a threat to anyone despite the circumstances that brought him here. Yes, Mr. Lewis did set fire to a building, but no one was injured. And he called the fire department himself before it got out of control, which helps his case and her argument immensely. He didn't put up a fight or show any aggression to the police when they arrived on the scene. She believes that her patient suffers from PTSD relating to his wife's recent death and the fire itself is not her main concern.

She'd be lying if she said the same thought hadn't crossed her mind since East Nashville started building all those ugly, ridiculously expensive homes known as "tall and skinnies" all over the place. Alice lives in the same home she grew up in on Porter Road; only a few blocks away from where the incident with Mr. Lewis occurred. Hadn't she put the evil eye on the very same lot just a couple of weeks ago? Not that she'd wished for the place to be vandalized, of course. Her childish hoodoo—when she was a kid, she really believed she had the touch—had been a last-ditch effort to keep the new owners of the property from tearing down that beautiful 1928 bungalow. It hadn't worked obviously (unlike the time she put the evil eye on Mark, the mean kid who stole her bicycle and caused him to wreck and break his ankle. Something her friends still talk about when they get together for a beer). The old house disappeared and not one, not two, but three tall and skinnies seemed to sprout up like weeds in its place overnight.

Alice still gets mad when she thinks about it. But that is not the issue here, she tells herself and refocuses on Mr. Lewis.

Alice smiles. It's a genuine smile, Alice feels a connection to her patient. There's something about him that seems familiar. He reminds her of the old guys who used to meet her uncle for a beer at Dino's or for a coffee and ham biscuit at the market on Greenwood Ave. But those places have changed. Her uncle would roll over in his grave if he could see them now.

She smiles and wills him to be the one to make the first move. He hasn't spoken a single word in the past twenty-four hours since being admitted to the psych ward. Nothing, not so much as a peep. Alice has worked with Alzheimer's patients who displayed similar symptoms, but Mr. Lewis doesn't have the wilted, lost look that goes with the disease. He seems strong—solid. Present, even though he's closed off. If she can just get him to speak.

Alice finally tires of the one-sided game of stare and looks down at her lap. She doesn't need to open his folder. Earlier that morning, she'd read everything about him before her coffee had a chance to turn cold in its cup. The folder is deceptively thin—her patient never had so much as a parking citation until the incident. But sadly, there's a lot of information on the few pages inside. In the last twenty-six months her new patient had lost his wife of forty-nine years to cancer. His daughter had moved across the state, and to top it all off, his dog, Chief, had recently crossed over the rainbow bridge. Mr. Lewis was the last of the original homeowners on his street. If what his daughter told her is accurate, everyone his age has either moved to a warmer climate, to an assisted living facility or died. In the brief phone consultation with the patient's daughter, the therapist concluded that Chief, an eighteen-year-old terrier of some sort, had been the patient's only friend left. There's no wonder her patient acted out. Everyone has a breaking point.

"Mr. Lewis, do you know why you're here?" she asks when it is obvious that Al isn't going to speak. Before either one of them knows what's happening, the old man is sobbing. No, sobbing isn't exactly what's happening. Her patient is wailing.

This is good, she thinks. Per his daughter, he's never grieved the death of his wife. Alice is willing to bet he'd never grieved the loss of Chief either. She believes that the unexpressed grief for his loved ones is all that is wrong with Frank Lewis.

Frank ignores the young doctor and wonders if he might be having a heart attack and welcomes the idea. He has no control over the flood of tears that pours from his eyes, or the way the muscles contort and pinch in his face. The pain comes from deep in his stomach, forcing its way into his chest. It feels as if his ribs might break before the pressure rises up his neck and pushes its way out of his mouth.

"Fucking hipsters ..." he says before another wail chokes off the rest of the sentence.

The young therapist's eyebrows are the only things that move. She quickly brings them back down and adjusts her glasses. This is not what she expected, but she's glad to hear his voice. She sits behind her poker face and waits for him to continue. Several minutes pass before she attempts to hand him the box of tissues. If he notices the tissues she offers, he ignores them. She pauses before deciding to put the box back on the table and starts to wonder if she heard him correctly. Hadn't she just said the same thing this morning as she jogged past Dino's? *Fucking hipsters,* she'd cursed under her breath as she ran past the litter of red plastic cups and cigarette butts left out on the sidewalk from last night's crowd.

Mr. Lewis continues to cry. This is going to take a while, she thinks and repositions herself, trying to get comfortable in the uncomfortable chair. She watches as the front of his shirt becomes soaked and feels that the show of emotions is definitely progress. Her colleagues had been certain that he wouldn't be able to communicate at all, that he isn't even aware of where he is or why. She disagrees.

The patient takes a deep breath, tries to open his mouth to speak, but his teeth are clenched so tightly together he can only continue to cry.

What good would it do anyway? Frank thinks. The

doctor looks like one of them.

Young, wealthy; wearing vintage glasses and her expensive suit. She probably lives in one of the new ugly houses with some guy who wears vests and skintight jeans and owns a tattoo parlor. She probably thinks he's some old fart that needs to be put in a home.

Hazel, I miss you so goddamned much. I tried to keep all of my promises to you. I even stopped swearing – well, almost. I keep your roses watered and trimmed, the grass mowed, the porch swept. Hazel. It makes me so goddamn mad I can't see straight. You wouldn't believe it. Hipsters they call themselves. Fucking hipsters. He almost chokes but pulls in another ragged breath and continues to cry with a vengeance.

Moving in from god knows where, taking over everything. Most of our friends have moved, Hazel. They couldn't afford the goddamn property taxes. Old Ethel held on as long as she could, God bless her, but her greedy kids got wind of those fucking hipsters swarming in like a bunch of locusts and convinced poor Ethel that her hip was just waiting to break. As soon as she signed the deed over to that no count red-neck son of hers, they moved her into a rundown old folks' home not fit for convicts or stray cats. They sold her house for half a million dollars – you heard that right Hazel, five hundred thousand – and the next thing you knew it was gone. Bulldozed over.

Ethel's house was the prettiest house on Fairwin Ave. Now an ugly modern piece of shit sits on top of where Ethel's peonies used to bloom. All the thick grass exchanged for gravel and cement.

If you could see those people, Hazel. They walk these "designer" dogs they call them — big, goofy things bred to not shed. What kinda dog doesn't shed? Walking around with their noses glued to their phones, letting their dogs shit wherever they feel like. Never picking up after them either. Hell, our dog, Chief — a real dog — would never even think of taking a dump in front of somebody's mailbox. Remember how he loved to walk to the market? Well, there ain't no more market, Hazel. The fucking hipsters turned it into some high- end butcher and cheese shop where you have to have a fucking trust fund to be able to afford a slice of goddamn cheese.

He pulls in a big breath of air and the therapist leans in. Frank manages to say, "Ignorant disrespectful sons of bitches ..." before another round of sobs take over.

The therapist doesn't have to wonder if she heard him correctly that time. Nope, she heard Frank Lewis loud and clear. She settles back in and makes a note in the file. It's not at all what she was hoping for, but at least he's talking.

Frank's comments remind her to call her friend

Laney. Alice had a bone to pick with her for giving her number to a guy a few nights before. She didn't know why she'd even gone with them to Dino's, she couldn't stand the place anymore. Alice had started a new game called, Hipster or Mennonite. It's not that she had anything against Mennonites, not at all, but these guys looked ridiculous—like they should be riding on a wagon behind a mule, not sitting on a barstool. Dark jeans with a wide cuff folded at the ankles, plaid shirts buttoned all the way to the top button and a pair of suspenders or a snug fitting vest. Everyone wanting to express their individuality by looking exactly alike. Alice can't see herself dating a guy who had a six inch handlebar moustache and only drank twelve-dollar craft beer.

Hazel, they turned my bar into some kind of overpriced, over- crowded joint where you can't even get a goddamned Miller High Life anymore. Smells like clove cigarettes and the goddamned barber shop, what with all that hair tonic they use. Fucking entitled assholes. The last time Frank went to Goodwill in search of a blanket for Chief's bed he'd witnessed two young women pushing past a poor old guy to grab a western shirt off the rack in front of him. They were yapping about how great the shirt would go with their designer jeans, not even noticing the look on the man's face. Frank had been so pissed he left without paying for his purchase and had to go back in to apologize.

I spend most of my time at home now. If I had a beer, I'd sit in the backyard in our swing. Chief and I liked to sit out there in the afternoons after I cut the grass or trimmed the hedges. From the swing I could still see where I carved our initials into the trunk of the big oak tree on our fifth anniversary. It still had the nest where the pair of doves came back each year to raise their clutches. But I can't even do that anymore.

She notices that Mr. Lewis tightens his fists as he squeezes his eyes tighter. She doesn't feel like she's in any danger, in fact she is silently cheering him on. She feels her own hands make small fists and takes a breath to relax, preparing for the man to unburden himself of two years' worth of grief. She knows that if he will just allow himself to talk about it, she can help him work through it. But he doesn't say anything else. He continues to suck in ragged breaths, not caring that he has a stream of snot running over his top lip. She feels he's close to a breakthrough and hopes that she's right, but it's hard to watch. Alice knows about grief; she still misses her aunt. She wants to tell Mr. Lewis that she understands, but she doesn't want him to feel like she's patronizing him. If only they could connect on some level…

She feels a vibration in her coat pocket and glances at her cell phone. *Goddamnit,* Alice grits her teeth as she hits decline. It's another one of those obnoxious contractors trying to get her to sell. They just can't get it through their thick skull that she is not interested in selling her house so they can turn it into some monstrosity like they did to the house next to hers. She used to sit on her back patio and drink her morning coffee while watching the sun come up, but after they tore down the house next door and built that new thing; her beautiful view is gone. Every single tree cut down with no thought about the squirrels and birds or anything else for that matter. A solid brick wall is in their place— the new house extends all the way to the back of the lot—two feet from Alice's fence and two stories above it. She named it the great wall of Texas when she found out the new neighbors were Dallas transplants.

Alice is quite sure they're the ones behind the phone calls after the first and last conversation she had with her new neighbors. She had welcomed them to the neighborhood and the first thing they asked her was if she was planning to sell this year. This year, like she was already packing. Alice had been dumbfounded, stood there blindsided while they told her their plans. They want more room for a two-car garage and a studio, apparently, he's a musician (no surprise to Alice since half of the newbies seem to think they will be the next new Nashville star) and

Alice's lot would be perfect for their addition.

Alice was livid. The new neighbors acted like her home was an eyesore. It isn't. It is a sweet little 1930's bungalow with all of the original woodwork, tile, and a working fireplace. It's a treasure, but what would they know? They tore down one just like it to build a concrete rectangle that looks like a warehouse. She grew up in that house with her Aunt Helen and when her aunt died, she left it to her. Alice promised her on her deathbed that she wouldn't sell. Even if she hadn't promised, her memories in that house are worth more than any dollar amount the house would bring. Plus, she's in great location—just a few miles from the hospital—with room for a garden and a yard full of trees. That house is her home.

As far as Alice is concerned, everyone trying to get her to sell can kiss her ass. She planted wisteria bushes to grow up her fence to block as much of the great wall as she can, knowing good and well that it's an invasive vine and will grow into her neighbor's yard. Passive aggressive maybe, but she felt better after her small act of rebellion. She's looking into getting chickens or goats, maybe a couple of big fat stinky potbellied pigs, for her back yard. Take that you entitled assholes.

Hazel, they tore down the house beside us and were putting up three in its place. Three. Ridiculous. I was doing my best to ignore it, but when they cut over on our property, tearing up the roots to our tree – breaking off the limb where the doves had made their nest.

"Do you know why you are here?" she asks again.

He never opens his eyes or stops crying, but he does nod. "You are not alone, Mr. Lewis." she says, thinking of all the patients his age that have lost their spouses. "There are many people that feel the same way you do."

Hazel, I am here in this office because when I came home to find that contractor in our backyard looking at our tree, shaking his head, I lost it. He started talking about an arborist – a goddamn arborist – for Christ's sake. Told me he would reimburse me for the cost of another tree. Like money was the answer. There's no amount of money to compensate for all the things I've lost. Two more feet and they would've dug into Chief – just two fucking feet.

I took my gas can and a box of kitchen matches and I went next door, sat right in the middle of one of those piece of shit prefab three-story things they're calling houses and lit that bastard on fire. I gathered all the mail together – all the hospital bills they're still sending me from when you were there, the statement from Mt. Olivet Cemetery, and the offers from all the different real estate agencies to buy our house. Fuck every one of them bloodsucking son of a bitches.

The hospital and the cemetery have already been paid in full – why do they keep sending me reminders that you're gone? I don't need anything to remind me of that, it's always on my mind. I put them in a paper sack so I could carry them in one hand and the gas can in the other. I know I did it. I meant to. I'm not going to lie. I'm not crazy like they think. I'm mad. So damn mad I can't see straight.

I have lost so much lately. Hazel, I miss you so goddamned bad it hurts but losing our town is too much to take. No one understands.

The young therapist can't stand it any longer. She reaches out to him and pats her patient's hand, feels encouraged when he doesn't pull away. If only she could find some common ground to start the conversation. Something besides the grief of their loved ones, some kind of bond. Alice doesn't want to come across as condescending, or authoritative. Mr. Lewis needs a friend more than anything. Alice knows that her way of treating her patients is frowned upon by some of her older colleagues, but she doesn't care. All she cares about is the man or woman that sits in front of her, and right now it's Frank Lewis. Once they find some common ground, the therapy can start. If she can just figure out what that is.

She tries once more to hand him the box of tissues,

but like the time before, he doesn't acknowledge it. She takes a deep breath and rephrases the question, "Will you tell me why you are here?"

He nods once again, and she sits up straighter.

He takes a deep breath at the exact same time Alice's phone buzzes. She barely glances at the number before she hits delete. It's another real estate agent; the one who sports a porkpie hat and plaid shirt (both two sizes too small) in his picture on the business card that keeps appearing in her mailbox. Alice memorized his number because she'd thought of calling him to tell him how ridiculous he looked and to demand he quit leaving his litter in her mailbox.

A whispered curse slips between her lips and she and Frank Lewis say in unison, "Fucking hipsters ..."

Waiting

"I don't even have a candle to keep me from freezing to death. Not one fucking candle. I can't wait any longer."

I pull into the lot, turn off the ignition and settle in to watch everyone walk through the double doors of the bus station. I'm not much interested about the people going in, just the ones coming out. Well, only one in particular, his name is Eddie. He's my boyfriend. Actually, I don't really know what he is anymore. It's complicated.

I park close so he can see my car—not like he could miss it. It sticks out like a sore thumb. It's an old Vega, covered with rust like most old Vegas, but what sets it apart is the piece of rope that sticks out of the passenger door. The other end of the rope goes back through a hole drilled in the side panel. That's to tie the door shut. Yep, you heard me. My passenger door is kept shut by a knot in a piece of rope. Oh, and there's the duct tape—I shit you not—taped around the window to keep the rain out. Hey, it works. My passenger seat has been dry ever since I found that roll of tape.

I got here early, in case his bus did too. If he got here before me, I didn't want him to think I'd given up on him. See, Eddie promised to be home about three weeks ago, but he admitted to me that he went on a bender and lost all sense of time. Which is understandable, considering the news I told him before he left—and the fact that he found his long-lost sister—two completely separate crazy stories. Each one of them enough to make the most stable person lose their mind momentarily.

That first night three weeks ago, I sat here for over an hour, worried that I'd been late, that I'd missed his bus and he'd gotten tired of waiting on me. I had no idea where he'd go, so I sat there, waiting in the parking lot. Expecting him to walk up, pissed off that I'd not been there. But a cop pulled up and scared me off. Not that he did anything to make me afraid, it's just that my car looks so suspicious I wouldn't have blamed him if he wrote me a ticket for sitting there so long.

I thought about it on the drive home and figured if Eddie's bus had come early and he'd left already, he wouldn't come back to the bus station, would he? I went home and fell asleep waiting for a phone call that came three days later.

* * *

The next time he was supposed to come home, I waited for about an hour and a half. I finally left because I had to get to work, I couldn't be late again. I didn't want to get demoted from cashier to bagger. His sister Allison, a.k.a. Sexy Lexy, called me later that night to tell me he'd gotten a gig, one that actually paid decent money. She said he'd gone to Flint the day before but would be back in Detroit on Monday. She said he would call me when he got back. I thanked her for letting me know and the call ended there. I'd wanted to ask her why he hadn't called me himself, ask her how he was, and if he'd mentioned me at all—but she hadn't sounded too friendly. I didn't know his sister at all—he didn't either, really. They were separated when they were very young and had lived in different foster homes growing up.

Talk about a crazy coincidence. Allison was a dancer

at The Booby Bungalow and Eddie's drummer, Mark, had hired her and two other girls to dance on stage at the club where they played. I thought that was pretty clever of Mark, even though I didn't like it too much. The idea of strippers dancing around Eddie while I was stuck here going out of my mind was almost enough to do me in. If I hadn't had so much to try to figure out already, it would have killed me. But Eddie sounded so pitiful when he called me and told me what was going on, I didn't have the heart to say anything about how I felt about the situation. Once he told me what happened, I felt sorry for him.

See, Eddie and Lexy found out they were long lost siblings while they were getting high in the alley. They were all swapping stories of their childhoods, the band and the dancers, of course. Who else would my boyfriend be smoking pot in an alley with, right? And Eddie said Lexy told them a story of her father driving up in a new truck, after being missing in action for a week. How her dad had showed up like nothing had happened with gifts for everybody. He brought a puppy for her, a dirt bike for her little brother, and a new microwave for their mother.

Eddie said it felt like he'd entered the twilight zone. He knew the story. Eddie said he told Lexy that the dog was a mutt, the dirt bike was a little Yamaha 70, and the microwave was as big as a hotel room refrigerator. Lexy flipped out and thought he was a stalker or wacko, until Eddie told her that she named the dog Jett, they only ate nuked hotdogs for lunch from then on, and that her little brother ran the dirt bike into the ravine two weeks after he got it. He pulled up his sleeve and showed her the scar to back up his story.

After the shock wore off, they laughed and then they cried together. They stayed up all night talking. But it really messed him up. I mean, could you imagine? He kept telling me over and over that he could've made out with her and not even known it was his sister. That he could have paid her for a lap dance like Mark had that first night. He said it made him sick—*that he'd seen her boobs*. He said there was nothing about her that reminded him of his sister Allison. Nothing. Not the color of her hair, or the way she yelled instead of talked. Not the look in her eyes, and definitely not in the way she strutted and bounced around like she wanted everyone to look at her.

Eddie said she used to walk on her tiptoes, like she was scared she'd make too much noise and get noticed. She'd changed her name to Lexy and had a Sexy Lexy tramp stamp inked on her lower back. A horrible tattoo that Eddie said looked like it'd been given with a homemade tattoo gun, the kind that you get in someone's garage in the middle of a party on a dare. He said she was completely fucked up. Eddie told me that he wasn't sure if he was happy that he found her or sad because he did. He told me he wanted to feel good being with family—real family—but she was a mess. That's all we talked about when he called me. He couldn't get his head wrapped around it. Then he said something that really got me. He couldn't believe that the only thing about him his sister recognized was his scar. He had no idea that he'd changed at all. Until then he thought everyone saw the same scared, scrawny kid he used to be. I guess that part is what got to me the most. Because when I looked at Eddie, I saw a grown man. I had no idea that he still felt like a kid.

Then he called me on Tuesday and said he'd be on the next Greyhound heading home, which would be the following Thursday. He told me it was a nonstop trip from Detroit to Nashville and he'd already bought the ticket. So here I am, waiting one more time. I feel like I have spent most of my life waiting on something to happen.

It's cold out here and there's no heater in this old piece of junk. I know it'd be warm inside the station, but I can't go in there. I can't stand the smell of a bus station. They all smell so sad to me, like stale vanilla wafers and cigarette butts. I hate them. Plus, I don't think I could take it if I were standing there waiting and he didn't get off the bus. I would rather be sitting in my own car, with the keys in the ignition. Luckily, I have a blanket in the backseat that Lucy, my little sister, and I took to the park the other night. We laid on it and stared at the stars. I almost told her then—almost, but she's just a kid. I am her big sister. I'm supposed to be the strong one. I couldn't tell her my problems; she's got enough of her own. She's a freshman this year— enough said. Besides, I couldn't stand to tell another person. Eddie is the only one who knows.

I grab the blanket and see my satchel on the floorboard behind the passenger's seat. I grab it too, hoping it held an apple, and a bottle of water. I read somewhere that you weren't supposed to refill the plastic bottles with tap water because the plastic let out cancer-causing particles. But I can't see paying a dollar when you can get it free, so I always refill them. Besides, have you seen the tap water that comes out of the faucets in Davidson County? I think the last thing you have to worry about is what plastic container you carry it in. It's a wonder the water doesn't eat through the bottle. I'm joking, of course. I'm always joking. That's my defense. No luck on the apple, but I do find a piece of gum, water, and the pamphlets from the health clinic.

All of a sudden I'm freezing. I place the satchel with the pamphlets stacked in a small pile on top in the passenger seat and cover myself with the blanket. I glance over at the stack of papers beside me.

Pro-Choice. Pro-Life. Wish I had more choices when it came to choosing *my* life.

I tuck the blanket under my legs and put my hands between my knees to warm them up and wait for Eddie. When I met Eddie, I was thirteen and he was fourteen. He'd transferred to our school in the middle of the year. He was skinny and shy, but tough. He had the biggest, darkest brownest eyes I'd ever looked into. And he didn't take any crap from anybody. He was the only person I'd ever met that lived in foster care. We had our first conversation, which turned into an argument in the library. We were both looking for stories on the Bell Witch. He didn't believe in her and I did. I'd just gotten back from Adams, Tennessee, and had seen the signs for her everywhere. We got into a heated discussion about whether she existed or not and Ms. Clark made the two of us sit in the hallway until it was time to go back to class. Eddie and I have been best friends ever since.

I found out a lot about Eddie that first year. I discovered that he'd been in foster care since he was seven years old. He'd been molested by his first foster dad, beaten by his second foster mom because he accused her husband of being a pervert like the first one, treated like a slave by the third family, and like the family pet by the fourth. He said he hated them all. Eddie said nobody ever cared to know him, nobody asked him any questions. Nobody paid attention. They all treated him like it was his fault he was in the system. That he must have been some kind of juvenile delinquent instead of a scared seven-year-old, orphaned by his parents. Eddie said even the ones who had been halfway decent acted like they were scared of him.

His birth parents never tried to get back with him and he didn't try to find them. He said the last time he saw them they were both drunk and fighting, each of them threatening to leave the kids with the other one. He had a sister, but he hadn't seen her since his eighth birthday. Eddie had described her as a nerdy, pimple-faced geek, but he made it sound like a compliment. He guessed she would go to college to be a teacher because she loved school. When they were little she'd rather stay at school than go home. She always had her nose stuck in a book, with her dark, plastic-framed glasses sliding off her face because they were so heavy. At first I thought that he was making fun of her, but then I realized he was bragging on her. Eddie wanted to believe that she was doing better than him, that was all. He used to say when we got married and had kids one day, he hoped to have a daughter just like her. He said she'd tried to be a mother figure for him even though she was only two years older than he was. I can understand why he was so hurt when he found her.

I learned I was pregnant the day before Eddie got the call to go to Detroit with his friends. He was pretty good on an electric guitar. That was his dream—to be the next Eddie Van Halen. As a matter of fact, his real name is Charles Edward. When I'd met him he went by Chuck, but then he heard Van Halen for the first time and changed his name to Eddie. I told him I was pregnant about twenty minutes before his phone rang.

We were sitting in silence while reality sunk in. He never said a word until he answered his phone.

Eddie went from total silence to complete frenzy in two minutes. He hung up the phone, pulled me up off the couch, and spun me around in a circle. For a second, I'm ashamed to admit, I thought he was happy for us. But that wasn't it. It was the phone call that had him so excited. It was a call for a gig somewhere up north for the following weekend. It sounded like good money and he'd only be gone for three days, five tops. He called a couple of his friends and seemed to forget about me. Like, completely forgot about what we'd been talking about. I watched his face; he was so happy. He was so excited. This was a big deal for him after all. His friend's band was pretty well known around here, but they were hoping to play some bigger venues. This was a great opportunity. How could I screw that up for him?

I decided to wait until he came home to talk about it again. I wanted to talk to him face to face, not over the phone. And I mean, seriously—I'd just found out. I was only, what, three weeks along at the most? It's not even a *real thing* yet, right? I could wait another week.

Well, the five-day gig turned into a two-week gig while I waited to hear from him and tried not to panic. When he called me fourteen days later, I told him we had to talk about the baby. Eddie refused to talk about it over the phone. He promised me that we would talk about it when he came home, and that he was coming home the following night. So I waited. That was the first time he stood me up. That was the night he found out that Sexy Lexy—the stripper with the ugly tattoo, nice boobs, and bag of weed—was actually his sister. He'd been so messed up he completely forgot about me.

I understood, I mean, I couldn't blame him. And anyway, he was coming back in two days so I could wait. What would another forty-eight hours matter, right? But when he called me to apologize for not coming home, I told him that we had to talk about *the thing* that we had to talk about. We couldn't put it off any longer. I couldn't bring myself to say the word *baby*. It didn't seem right. I mean a baby shouldn't be something that's ignored, and so far that's exactly what Eddie had been doing. I told him the longer we waited, the fewer choices we'd have.

He asked what I meant by choices. Eddie got agitated and said he could not be responsible for killing an innocent baby. He said if that's what I wanted to do, then that would be my decision. That was my choice, not his. My choice. That he wanted to do the responsible thing. When I asked what the responsible thing was, Eddie had no reply, other than to wait for him to come back before I made any decisions. So I waited for him the second time and that's when I got the call from Lexy.

The last time I talked to him was two nights ago. He swore to me that he was coming home and that we would sit down and figure everything out. After that call, I went to the clinic and picked up the brochures on abortion, adoption, and anything else I could find that I thought might help us "figure it out." I wanted to have all the bases covered.

But if anything, I was more discouraged. The Pro-Choice pamphlets said that this was my life—my life—my choice. But the Pro-Life pamphlets said it was not my life. It's some unborn person's life.

And I'm the one who has to figure out how to take care of myself and this other life. What does it want? Does it want to be in foster care? Does she or he want to live on Medicaid, treated like white trash? Does it want to be put up for adoption? Does it want a mother who drives a rusted-out old car with the door tied shut? A mother who doesn't have a high school diploma because she has to work two jobs to be able to afford to the cost of day care.

Does this baby want a father who resents it because he had to quit playing music to go to work framing houses or digging ditches to make the money to support it? Do I want to be responsible for *that*? Are those *my* choices?

I don't have anybody to talk to because I don't want to talk about it with anyone but Eddie. The way I see it, it is nobody's business but ours. He should be a part of the decision since whatever I do affects him too. I shouldn't have to decide his future. I can't be responsible for him, hell, I can't even be responsible for me. If I stay in school, I'll graduate in a year. School is easy for me. My job at Piggly Wiggly doesn't pay much but I am able to save a little each paycheck. And I will be eligible for the Hope Scholarship to apply towards tuition if I go straight into college. But I won't be able to take a year off to save more money or I'll lose it. If I can keep my grades up, I should be able to apply for more.

It would be hard, but I could do it. I could go to college like my mama wants me to. I could do it without putting a burden on her.

If I had a baby, I wouldn't be able to even think about college unless I asked mama for help and she's done nothing but help everybody her whole life. She's never been able to live her life for herself. Ever. I couldn't ask her to give up another six or seven years so I could have mine. She still has my little sister to raise.

I couldn't ask my father, that's a laugh. He's done nothing but complain about how much we've cost him since he and my mother divorced. He's fought her tooth and nail over child support and medical bills. The last birthday card I got from him and his new wife was empty.

I guess they've decided I'm too old for presents. Or that the monthly child support check that my mama uses towards the rent is a big enough gift to me. Whatever.

I don't want to give this baby up for adoption. What if it's got something wrong with it and nobody wants it? Or worse, its disabilities are used against it and it's turned into some kind of martyr for some attention seeking weirdos? What if it's put into foster care? What if it ends up in a foster home like Eddie's first one and ends up being molested? I can't do it. I can't take that chance. I can't make that decision alone.

I realize I'm seriously freezing when my teeth start chattering. This old rust bucket doesn't have a heater, but I do have a candle. I read somewhere—but I can't remember where—that if you become stranded in your car on an icy road, you can keep from freezing to death by the heat of one candle. I stuck a couple of candles in the glove box the same day I read the article and have used one. It works—I haven't frozen to death yet. Well, I've never been stranded in a snowstorm, but still, you get my drift.

I put the last candle on the dashboard and reach deep into the front pocket of my jeans for a lighter. It's the only thing I have that belongs to Eddie. I took it the day he left. Slid it into my pocket without saying anything while he was on the phone with one of his friends. I felt silly at the time, wanting something that was his, but I'm glad I have it now.

I try to get a flame and it won't even spark. Go figure. After three tries I start to give up, but finally I get a spark and feel hopeful. This is good because it's getting bad outside, the wind is really picking up. I can tell by the way it sounds as it pushes its way through the holes in the passenger side door, like some eerie calliope in a Stephen King movie. But then I almost lose all hope when nothing happens on tries ten and eleven. My eyes fill up with water, but I force myself to swallow the lump in my throat. I have been holding it all together and I am not going to lose it over some goddamn piece of shit Bic lighter. I hear the wind pushing against the glass, trying to get through the strips of duct tape and slide its icy fingers down the neck of my jacket. The thought makes me shudder, but it also pisses me off enough to stop the tears from starting.

Finally, after fifty or more tries, the spark catches and I have fire. I grab the candle and stop breathing until the wick takes hold and lights. After placing the candle on the dashboard, I flip a bird through my windshield. Fuck you, wind, I win this round. I think of the women and girls who were at the clinic earlier today, waiting to see the doctor.

Everyone looked so scared and alone. Or so sad it about broke my heart. But there were two girls who were talking to each other and didn't care that everyone could hear them. They were arguing over the cost of abortion versus giving your baby up for adoption and it sounded like they were each trying to convince the other to change their mind. What I gathered from their conversation it cost about four hundred dollars to abort—but if you had your baby and couldn't afford the cost of the hospital stay and left your baby in state custody, it wouldn't cost you anything. One of them said that she thought she could actually make money if she put it up for adoption. I wanted to say to them that they should put both of their babies on eBay and sell them to the highest bidder. Highest bids wins. But instead I sat there and tried to tune them out. I wanted to get the hell out of there, they made me itchy and even more ashamed to be there than I already was.

When the nurse finally called me back, I caught a glimpse of my reflection in the mirror hanging in the hallway. I looked at the girl in the reflection and realized she was no different than every other female out in the waiting room. How had that happened?

* * *

I reach over and pick up one of the Pro-Choice/Planned Parenthood pamphlets I took from the clinic and start reading. *Abortion is an integral part of reproductive health care.* That sounds pretty reasonable. *Abortions are safe; the risk of death from childbirth is eleven times greater than the risk of death from an abortion procedure during the first twenty weeks of pregnancy.*

That's good to know. Unless I decide to give birth…then not so much.

Aspiration abortion – the most common kind of in-clinic abortion. An aspiration procedure takes approximately five to ten minutes. Are you serious? It only takes five to ten minutes to finish the procedure? *But more time may be needed to prepare your cervix. Time is also needed for talking with your provider concerning the procedure, a physical exam, reading and signing forms, and a recovery period of about one hour.* Well, I'd hope so, jeez.

You may have cramps after an abortion. You will probably want to relax for the rest of the day. You can usually return to work or other normal activities the next day. If I had it on Friday, I would miss only one day of school and two days of work.

Safety is an important and common concern for women. In-clinic abortion procedures are very safe. But there are risks with any medical procedure. The risks increase the longer you are pregnant. I don't have much time to waste.

Nationwide, the cost at health centers ranges from three hundred and fifty to nine hundred dollars for abortion in the first trimester. I have twelve hundred dollars hidden in my sock drawer for college.

Serious, long-term emotional problems after abortion

are about as uncommon as they are after giving birth. Whatever. *A tube is inserted through the cervix into the uterus. Either a hand- held suction device or a suction machine gently empties your uterus.* Ugh. I have a flash of a TV commercial for a Hoover vacuum showing how the little brush attachment safely removes dust from sheer curtains.

You can feel confident in knowing that these abortion methods are very effective. They work almost every time they are done. Almost? *Almost?* Okay, enough of that.

I look at my watch. Eddie's bus must be running late. Good thing I have something to keep me occupied. I pick up a Pro- Life pamphlet I'd snatched from the same shelf that held the Pro-Choice information. *Complications you can have with your abortion. Bladder injury, bowel injury, breast cancer: Women who have aborted have significantly higher rates of breast cancer later in life. Breast cancer has risen by 50 percent in America since abortion became legal in 1973.* Because of abortion? Bullshit. I pick up my cancer-causing plastic water bottle and take a drink.

Ectopic (tubal) pregnancy, effects on future pregnancies, failed abortion, hemorrhage, hepatitis infection, laceration of the cervix, retained products of conception. If your doctor leaves pieces of the baby, placenta, umbilical cord, or amniotic sac in your body, you may develop pain, bleeding, or a low-grade fever. Besides antibiotics and possible hospitalization, you may require additional surgery to remove these remaining pieces. Okay, okay—it's a serious process.

NO SHIT. But I'm not worried about me, I'm worried about whether a baby I give birth to will be fed, clothed, loved. A little hemorrhaging or cervical laceration doesn't scare me. Bring it on.

Day 1: Conception: Of the two hundred million sperm that try to penetrate the mother's egg cell, only one succeeds. At that very moment, a new and unique individual is formed. Let's see, I am about what, five weeks along?

Day 28-32: Two tiny arms make their appearance and budding legs follow two days later. The beginnings of the mouth take shape. The nose starts to develop. The thyroid gland begins to grow. Blood flows in the baby's veins but stays separate from the mother's blood. The tongue now begins to form. The face now makes its first appearance. Does it looks like me? Or does it look more like Eddie?

There is not a legitimate "pro-choice" position that can be derived from the Bible. Don't even get me started. Where were all the bible-thumping do-gooders when Eddie was being molested? When he kept being passed around from one abusive place to the other?

Abortion is No Minor Decision. Really? You think I

haven't gotten that?

Any minor considered mature enough to make this grave decision is certainly old enough to care for the child she carries. Old enough—I am way older than my seventeen years, but what the hell does that have to do with being able to care for a baby—to provide for it? To be able to protect him or her? I can't think about this anymore, I'm too tired. My head is killing me and I'm hungry. I close my eyes and let the weight I've been carrying on my shoulders slide down my chest and rest in the middle of my ribcage. It's so heavy, it feels like it could stop my heart from beating. But it won't. Nothing could get past the walls I've built around that piece of muscle. I wouldn't know how to let something in even if I wanted it to.

* * *

I must've fallen asleep because the same cop from the last time is here, pounding on my window. He shines a light in my face, but I can't move. I realize I'm shaking and notice that the candle has burned out. All that's left of it is a few drips that ran down the dash, already solid and ice cold.

The cop opens my door—it's easy since there is no

lock—and shines the light across the interior of the car. I follow his gaze to the pamphlets strewn all over and start thinking of how to defend myself. He surprises me when he puts his hand on my shoulder.

"Are you all right, miss?" I can't open my mouth to answer.

Am I all right? Will I ever be all right again? When was the last time I felt all right? But he's patient. "It's way too cold to be sitting out here, you'll freeze to death. Are you waiting on someone?"

I look at my watch and see that I have been sitting here for over two hours. "I am. His bus must have been delayed or something. I guess I'll go see," I stammer and start to get up, but he keeps his hand on my shoulder and I don't have the energy to push it away.

"Do you have any identification?" I stare at him and realize I don't even know who I am anymore. I am not the same girl I was a month ago.

"Do you have a license?" He is looking straight into my eyes, and his eyes are kind. I struggle to get my wallet out of the bag buried under all the pamphlets. My fingers are so cold they're stiff so it's a slow process. I feel like I am moving underwater. Could I have actually frozen to death? Wouldn't that solve everything? The thought scares the shit out of me. I try hard to shake the feeling as I hand the police officer my driver's license. It's still there as I watch his reflection in the rearview mirror as he walks to his car.

After a few minutes he comes back and hands me my ID. "Here, take this." He offers me an official-looking business card. It has his name, Officer Paul Malloy, and two phone numbers on it. "Call either one of these numbers if you need my assistance." I seriously almost lose it then. It is all I can do to keep from bawling like a baby. I know that he is a police officer and it's his job to look out for lost souls, but he offered me more than anyone else has in a long time. Call if you need my assistance.

I take his card and try to hide the tears behind a smirk. "Thanks. And you know what, Officer? It looks like a piece of crap, but it does run."

Officer Malloy nods once, tells me to be safe, and walks away. He turns around to say something else but must've thought better of it. I sigh a breath of relief. I can only take so much kindness from a stranger. It's hard when you aren't used to it.

I stand there by my car for a second while I work up the nerve to go inside the station. I hate to walk through those doors. I hate, hate, hate bus stations. I hate them more than any other place in the world. I remember standing with my mama and my baby sister in one a lifetime ago. Our father had dumped us off with only one suitcase for the three of us and enough money for the tickets to get us to my grandmother's house in Indiana. Not a penny more.

My mama did not shed a single tear at that station. She waited until hours later, when she thought we were asleep. She didn't cry until she and my grandmother sat down at the kitchen table. I heard my grandmother tell her that everything would be okay. She told mama that she'd made it when her husband, my grandfather, left them and mama would make it too. It seemed like mama cried for the next four months straight. Once she finally started it was hard for her to stop.

I walk to the counter to see what the delay is all about. It takes me a minute to understand what the person behind the counter is saying to me. I know he must think I'm high or stupid because I make him repeat it three times. There is no bus coming in from Detroit tonight. There has not been a bus coming from Detroit anytime in the last three weeks. There are no nonstop bus routes from Detroit to Nashville.

I walk back out to the car in a daze.

A woman has a right to choose what she will with her own body. This is not a choice I want to make. This is not a choice that I want to make on my own. I am not choosing what I will do with my body—I am trying to make the right decision for someone else. Someone who can't speak for themselves, someone who has no rights, and someone who could very possibly NEVER have any rights. It could be given the kind of life where there are no options, no choices—no chances. Should I make the choice to force this child on Eddie, when he can't even face *talking* about it? Look at my father—he didn't want me or my sister and he loved our mother at one time. Eddie doesn't have a clue what love is. Wouldn't he resent it for the rest of his life? I wish it was as simple as choosing what I want. If it were that easy, I'd have this baby. I'd have this baby and we'd have a car with a heater. Fuck. We'd have one with a door handle. Hey, if I'm wishing for what I want, might as well reach for the stars, right? If it were just me, just my life, and not another human being's life that I am choosing what to do with, then it would be easy. But it's not that simple. This is a decision that affects not only me, but Eddie, and an *unborn fetus.*

As I open the door to my car I notice that it has started to snow. I don't even have a candle to keep me from freezing to death. Not one fucking candle. I can't wait any longer.

* * *

If more people who considered themselves pro-lifers, were as sincere about saving the unborn person's life as they were about the birth, then maybe I could believe that there's hope that this baby wouldn't end up another statistic. But I know for a fact that many people who call themselves "pro-life" would flip the switch to fry someone less fortunate if they thought that person was costing them a cent of their hard-earned money. Last month, those same types of people cut the funds for the free lunch program at Lucy's school. They talk the talk, but they don't walk the walk.

How many homeless people in America, how many young men stuck in prison, how many teenage girls who sell them- selves for drugs—the same people who are considered the lowest of the low, a disgrace to the working class—were once little innocent babies that the "pro-life" people considered another victory? A victory at first, but then left to fend for themselves once they're old enough to be forgotten about.

I know what it's like to be judged by the clothes you wear and the house that you live in. I've watched my mother struggle my whole life. Her father left her when she was a baby and she never got over it. She always thought it was her fault, that she was unlovable. She never remarried after my father left us—she blamed herself for everything, even after he screwed up two more marriages.

I don't want to be the reason why it, this unborn baby, this little thing who doesn't *even know what desperation is*, has to live a life of heartache and disappointment. I can't make that decision. I can't *choose* that.

I put my keys in the ignition and pick up the Pro-Choice (what a stupid name) pamphlet and make a circle around the contact number on the back page.

I finally let the tears fall that I've been holding back for weeks, not worrying anymore if I'll ever stop crying. What does it matter anyway? I let them run in icy rivers down my cheeks and soak the front of my jacket.

Tomorrow, I'll stop waiting

Her Baby Will Sing

"She remembered every word in the old songs she used to sing with her mother. It was a wonderful feeling. Her baby would sing."

When True woke to the cry of a feral rooster she had a moment of panic. The shadows cast unfamiliar shapes against the low ceiling and corners of her room. The mattress underneath her felt like a living thing that wanted to swallow her whole. For a moment, she didn't know where she was. True threw the quilt to the floor and struggled to get to the side of the bed but became tangled in her flannel gown. She felt a scream working its way up her throat when the rooster crowed again. It shook True out of her panic and back to the present. She was in her cabin. She was alone and she was safe.

True rubbed the sleep from her eyes and turned towards the window while she waited for her heart to settle down. Another rebel yell from the rooster. She peered around the room and shook her head at how different everything looked at that hour. True was usually up before the chickens, halfway through her morning chores before there was a peep from the wild things that roosted in the pines.

She chided herself for being so childish, then got up to start her day.

But something *was* different. At first, she blamed the odd feeling on the fact that she'd slept so soundly—the deep indention in the feather mattress proof that True hadn't moved a muscle during the night. But it was more than that. It took her awhile before she understood exactly what the feeling was. She felt different, lighter. She realized the weight she'd carried on her shoulders for so long was no longer there. True noticed as she emptied the ashes from the fireplace that she could actually stand up straight. She could take a deep breath and let it out without the familiar catch in her chest, drawing her shoulders in. She stood a little taller and drew in as much air as her lungs could hold but still no tightness, no pinch in her rib cage.

True stretched and winced at the sore muscles in her back and arms. She remembered her mother telling her that if you woke up with sore muscles it meant you'd fought the devil in your dreams. Her father, the practical one, said they were growing pains. True thought she'd passed the age to have growing pains and reckoned she was achy from sleeping so heavily. But the other feeling, the feeling of lightness, held her attention.

Why today?

He hadn't come home but that was nothing new, her husband would stay gone for days at a time. But the night before was the first time she'd slept through without waking up, wondering if he'd be coming in with liquor on his breath and an attitude to match the miserable smell.

Funny, I hadn't thought about him once last night.

True finished up the chores inside and went out to take care of the animals. The sun peeked over the mountains with a promise of blue skies, but it would be awhile before the shadows lifted completely from her cabin. The cabin sat in a small vale, protected by the harsh winds in the winter and kept cool in the summer by hills on each side. On the left, the hill sat farther back which allowed the sun to hit the pasture. The fields in the back were level and open. Her father had built the cabin himself with pines he cleared from the property. A gift to her mother before he asked her to marry him.

Trudy Elizabeth—True for short— was born and raised

there and when her parents died it was left to her. Well, it used to be hers; now it was her husband's. Everything was his, even her. He'd made that clear more times than she could count. The last time while pushing her face down onto the solid wood of the kitchen table, the table her father had built when True was just a child. The same table where she served his meals.

But True's husband had no sentimental attachment to the piece of furniture, not caring if he scratched or gouged the wood. Not caring if he bruised her cheekbone or split her lip against it. Not caring that the edge of the table left bruises on her thighs and hips and a shame that lingered with every meal served. But that was the least of True's worries. In a few months, seven if she'd done the math correctly, there would be another person her husband would take claim of if she didn't figure out a way to stop him.

When she poured what little slop she had for the hogs into the trough, she had a faint memory of the dream from the night before.

Or was it from the night before that?

The memory made her shudder, a horrible dream she didn't want to remember.

How can some dreams seem so real?

After the hogs were fed, she milked the scrawny cow. True studied the bony, tired-looking animal, and scratched behind its ear. Raising her arm reminded her of her sore muscles. True squeezed her right bicep with her left hand and grimaced. It felt like she was made of gristle and bone. She looked at the cow and shook her head.

Poor little thing, I know just how you feel.

Finished with the milking, True turned the cow out to graze. Then she let the mule out of the lean-to into the pasture on the left of the property to try to find something to eat in the melted patches of snow. This was her favorite part of the property, where she would grow her sunflowers come spring. She'd grown them for years, like her mother had when True was a little girl. The big yellow flowers kept the birds out of the garden and helped to bring in some extra money for the few things she bought from town. Everyone looked forward to the salty sunflower seeds True sold in the summer. She used her mother's secret and added cayenne pepper to the salt mixture when she laid them out to dry.

She loved that field of sunflowers. It was a beautiful place to go and think. When she was young, she dreamt of getting married to a man like her father and having a dozen children. They would run wild and free without a worry in the world, surrounded by the bright yellow petals. True used to watch her mother work in the flowers, wearing her bonnet and always smiling. She spent hours as a little girl daydreaming about her babies playing there one day.

Now she loved her field of sunflowers for another reason. They offered a place for her to hide. If he was drunk enough, he couldn't find her out there. But only if he was drunk enough. Most of the time he was just drunk.

True tucked her hair behind her ear and changed the direction of her thoughts. She knew if she kept busy it would keep the bad feelings away. She finished the laundry and hung it on the line to dry.

If he comes home tonight, he'll be expecting a meal on the table.

She went down to the root cellar and collected a couple of potatoes from a burlap bag hung beside the door on an old horseshoe nail. She folded up the front of her dress to make a pocket, then scooped some dried beans from another burlap bag into a coffee can. True set the can between the potatoes in the front of her dress and left the cellar. She carried her loot to the smokehouse to cut a piece of salt pork for seasoning.

When True picked up the large butcher knife they kept out there for slicing pieces of the cured meat, her hand shook. Her stomach turned as she slipped the sharp blade through the piece of salted pork and she fought the urge to vomit. It never bothered her before. But she gagged as the blade touched a piece of bone and almost dropped the corner of her dress. She quickly finished the task.

Maybe the baby makes me feel this way.

Something told her that wasn't it, but she forced that thought out of her mind like she had the dream. She didn't have time to worry about those things. She had too much work to do.

The baby. If her memory was correct, she was two months along.

A baby.

After her husband showed his true side, she thought there was no way she could ever be a mother. They could barely survive the winters themselves, not to mention her husband's mean streak and unpredictable temper. Life with him was too hard, too unpredictable. To bring a baby into it would've been selfish and wrong. She'd been so careful, or so she thought, but she understood there were some things she had no control over. Maybe it wasn't up to her if she got pregnant, but it was up to her to protect the life growing inside her. Even more so once it was born. She wouldn't let this baby suffer through life. She would give it all the love it needed to grow up strong and healthy. True thought of one of her mother's sayings.

Where there's a will there's a way.

Her mother also used to say that God takes care of his

children. True had her doubts about that, but maybe the baby was a sign.

Maybe He finally remembered me here in this little cabin.

True went into the kitchen and removed the cast iron pot she used for stew and beans from its hook over the stove. She walked outside and filled the pot with clear spring water from the well. True stopped on the path, stretched her back and smiled at the way it felt to hold her shoulders straight without the pinch in her chest. Back inside, she started a fire in the stone fireplace and hung the pot on the metal hook above it. Next, she peeled and cut the potatoes to put with the beans and pork. She liked the way it felt, having a pot of beans cooking in the kitchen. It was something solid, something she could depend on. No matter how bad things could be, there were always beans for the pot and wood for the fire.

You have to be grateful for what you have.

Her mother used to sing as she did her chores. She sang up until the day she died. Her mother had always been happy, even when things were hard. True wanted so bad to be like her, but her husband was nothing like the man her father had been. True hadn't felt like singing in years. But she surprised herself with a small hum that turned into song. She remembered every word in the old songs she used to sing with her mother. It was a wonderful feeling, singing and dancing around the cabin while she swept.

Her baby would sing.

True came across her husband's boots behind the door.

Odd, why are his boots here?

A wave of nausea hit her, and she closed her eyes to fight it. A flash of the dream ran across the back of her eyelids and that unsettling feeling tried to come back. It crept up her neck and down her spine, but True pushed it away before it took hold. She opened her eyes, straightened her back, and sang.

True finished sweeping and carried the boots out to the back porch, running her fingers over the soft leather. He always wore nice boots. True made do with his old hand-me-downs. Socks stuffed in the stretched- out toes so they wouldn't slip and leave blisters on her heels. She wondered what the new ones would feel like on her feet.

Soon it would be time to mix the batter for the corn cakes he always expected to have with his meal. But True was tired of corn cakes. She craved a big cathead biscuit like her mama used to make. Crispy on top and fluffy in the middle.

Tonight I think I'll make biscuits instead.

That sounded better and something told her he wouldn't be home for dinner. She couldn't help but smile as she cut lard into the flour and mixed up the dough.

* * *

A couple of months passed without any sign of him. True had biscuits as often as she liked, she sang every beautiful hymn and funny limerick she could remember and if she couldn't recall the words, she made up a few of her own. She'd recently taken her father's fiddle down from the mantel. Even though no one had touched it in a long time it sounded just as pretty as True remembered.

Thank God he never thought of it, or he would've traded it off for moonshine or whatever else he wanted. Like another pair of soft leather boots.

She was surprised to find that she could still remember a couple of tunes, and the more she played the better she sounded. Her father would've been proud.

Sometimes at night that old nightmare still reared its ugly head. The one where the snow was bright red, stained with blood. Her two hogs were loose in the yard, squealing and rooting around in the snow. True watched herself in the dream as if she was perched up in one of the trees looking down at herself. She watched as she carried a pair of boots into the house and saw that there was blood on her dress—a dress she hadn't seen since last winter. It made no sense to her, and it disturbed her so much, she didn't try to figure it out. She did her best to forget it.

One evening in early spring her neighbor, Mabel, came over with a box of baby things. She'd been blessed with five beautiful babies of her own. The fifth was her last Mabel said, and she wanted to give the things to someone who could use them. It felt right, the lady told the young mother-to-be, and that was that. In all the years they'd lived next to each other Mabel had only come by once before. True had been so embarrassed she'd wanted to die.

Her husband had been in the middle of one of his rants and had pulled True out into the yard, convinced she'd stolen his moonshine. True had tried to tell him that he'd hidden it in a different spot the week before, but he wouldn't listen.

Not only had Mabel witnessed True getting a beating with the horsewhip, True's husband threatened to give her a lashing for trespassing on their property. She couldn't believe that Mabel had come back, but there she was.

Before she left Mabel turned to True and said, "I'll return to check on you in a couple of weeks. And I'll be here when it was time for your baby to be born."

True was surprised at the woman's straightforward way, but she was so thankful, she could hardly speak.

"Thankee kindly." True managed to say before she was overcome with gratitude and hugged her neighbor there on the porch. No one, other than her parents, had been so nice to her.

Mabel had returned the hug and said, "You are not alone anymore." Then she whispered over True's shoulder, "You are one of the bravest women I've ever met."

True pondered on that, not sure what to make of it.

Before Mabel left, she also told True, "I've got a pair of shoes that'll fit you better than those boots. I'll send one of my girls over with them tomorrow. And you know, now's a good time to burn that brush pile out yonder." When True didn't respond, Mabel took hold of True's hands and gave them a gentle squeeze.

With one eyebrow slightly raised she'd looked True dead in the eye, nodded, and said, "A good time to burn any trash you might want to get rid of. I'd start with those boots."

True also pondered on that, but not as long.

* * *

When the time came, she worked the field by herself to get it ready for her sunflowers. Even though she was six months into her pregnancy, True was amazed at how easy it went. The mule—who she named Jake, seemed to do

242

all the work for her. Her husband had hated him. He'd kicked and cussed that old mule every day he worked him, calling him a worthless animal and threatening to shoot him at least once a week. But he seemed to love to pull the plow for her.

Maybe because True took the time to scratch Jake's ears and fed him apples from the orchard instead of kicking and cussing. Maybe because she'd given him a name. The apples were a new treat for the hogs as well. She thought the sow, Miss Gertie, looked fatter and healthier than ever. Her husband would've never allowed it, feeding the animals something as good as that, said it was a waste. Even though so much fruit went bad, rotting on the ground, he refused to let the animals have any.

True took pride in how healthy the animals looked. Miss Gertie especially. She'd given birth to a litter of twelve piglets and they had not only survived, they had grown into fat healthy pigs. In the past the few scrawny babies Miss Gertie had never lasted long. Her neighbors let her cow, which she'd named Minnie, out into the pasture with their bull. Mabel said True would have some beef come winter, but True knew she wouldn't be able to take the calf away from its mama. She didn't worry about it, she just enjoyed watching her fat happy cow, who used to look so unhealthy, make her way across the field to all the clover and hay she could eat.

True was content with the rabbits and venison her neighbor's brother brought over for her on occasion. Well, he would leave them with his sister. He would never be as forward as bringing it to her cabin, not wanting to imply that she couldn't take care of herself after she refused his offer to help with the plowing.

Her neighbor's brother. Just the thought of Jeremiah made her cheeks burn. Mabel told True that Jeremiah came down to help them when her husband broke his leg the year before. He'd told his sister that he fell in love with the mountain and decided to stay. Mabel had grinned and told True that she thought her brother had fallen in love with a mountain *girl*, and that's why he hadn't left.

True laughed at Mabel when she teased her about Jeremiah, but she often daydreamed about what it would be like to have someone like him. Someone to share her days with. A sweet man who left bundles of wild roses on True's porch when she was out in the garden. Too shy to give them to her in person, she'd find the roses tied with scraps of ribbon when she went in for dinner after working in the garden. The day he brought her a robin's egg she'd surprised him by coming in early. They'd both jumped and laughed at the startled looks on each other's faces. Then Jeremiah cleared his throat and held his hand out to True to show her the treasure he'd found.

"For some reason this made me think of you."

Jeremiah told her as his face turned a deep shade of red. "I think it's an omen that your baby is going to be a boy."

True remembered how he laughed at himself about the omen and how he'd turned his hat around and around in his hands. How he'd looked at her for a long time and smiled. True had never had anyone look at her like that. She'd made a nest with the scraps of ribbon from the roses for the robin's egg and placed it on her mantel. She had so much to be grateful for. Her small vegetable garden thrived. This time she did it her way, with wildflowers planted all around the borders. Maybe it was a waste of time, but the flowers were pretty, and she didn't mind the extra work it took to keep the weeds around them under control. She was sure they helped to keep the critters out of the vegetables, too, so it wasn't all a waste. Her husband would've called it horseshit and chopped them all down, but she hadn't seen hide nor hair from him since last November.

Or was it December?

She couldn't remember. She didn't think about him much anymore. His memory, like the bad dream, was as harmless as ashes in a burn pile. Ashes left behind from a pair of boots and a bloody dress, scattered down the mountain by now; swallowed up by kudzu vines and sweet honeysuckle. True cherished her new friends and their large, loving family. They'd taken her in and made her one of their own.

She rubbed her round stomach and felt a feeling so strong it brought tears to her eyes. Soon she would hold him in her arms. She would never let anyone harm this child. She smiled when the baby kicked and answered him back.

Yes, you love me too. You will be the happiest baby ever born in these mountains.

She'd baked a pie earlier to take with her to Mabel's, using the apples she canned last fall.

Last fall. That seemed like a hundred years ago. For some reason she thought of the piglets her sow had produced, how each one of them survived the harsh season. True couldn't help but smile as she ran her hand across her stomach. Her baby had survived as well.

True took a deep breath and closed her eyes. Her kitchen smelled like cinnamon and sugar. She no longer smelled the sweat and meanness that used to cling to the walls. No matter how hard True had scrubbed the pine planks, she could never get that smell out of there. His smell used to suffocate her.

But now, it was completely gone. She'd not even noticed it wasn't there until she smelled the fresh pie sitting on the table.

True stood up straight, took a deep breath without one single catch in her chest, and she smiled.

He Writes

*"...he'll write on anything he can find, using the
walls when there is nothing left."*

He writes, my father, filling each piece of paper using
a No. 2 lead pencil until he wears the point down to a nub.
When the urge hits him, he will go through a box of pencils
in no time at all. If he runs out of paper before he's run out
of words, he'll write on anything he can find, using the
walls when there is nothing left.

Countless times I've found him sitting in front of the
huge picture window in the near darkness. Unwilling—or
unable—to stop writing to turn on a light once the sun has
set.

His stories used to make the reader stop and laugh;

slow down and reflect on days gone by. Wholesome stories about old men who sit at the town square playing checkers. Whittling sticks down to splinters, spitting tobacco, and talking about the weather. Simple tales about old women who sit at kitchen tables, drinking coffee. Women sneaking cigarettes, talking about old men at the town square. Stories about kids at the park and the looks on their faces as their fathers push them as high as they dare in swings that creak and sway and cause their mothers to hold their breath until they are once again standing safely on the ground.

He would write about near-tame squirrels who steal crumbs from pigeons. Pigeons who still manage to look regal, strutting around, even though they are pecking and scratching with little bushy-tailed rodents. He would write about how the sun shines down through the leaves making sunlight dance on all the mothers, fathers, children, and funny old men, the squirrels and the pigeons. Making everything magical and mysterious like only he could do. There was a time when my father's stories were in high demand. He never made a fortune, mind you, but we lived comfortably, and our house was filled with his inspiring stories that were full of hope and simple pleasures that make life worth living.

Everyone loved to read my father's stories when he

used to write for pleasure, for the love of the written word. Now there is no pleasure or love to be found in his stories. His writing has become a dark obsession.

He used to write about dancing with a red-haired girl on the side of the road because the song playing on the car radio was just the right song. But now he writes about war, about fighting and death. About nightmares and nonsense. He writes about shame and confusion, lies and deception. He writes about pain. He writes about loss.

There used to be endless stories about the day the skinny, naïve writer married the beautiful red-haired girl. Sweet stories about the day her father took him aside, giving him a pocket watch that belonged to his own father. How it felt to be accepted, loved. How he made a promise to the red-haired girl's father to take care of his daughter and keep her from harm. Now he writes about broken promises. He used to write about the house on Elm Street where he—the skinny, naïve writer and my mother—the round, red-haired girl painted a little room bright yellow. How they and waited for their baby to finally make its appearance. Now he writes about hopelessness.

There are old pages written about me. Pages and pages of stories written about the daughter of the red-haired girl and the skinny, naïve writer, who got his blonde hair and her freckles. Pages written about my first day at school, how my mother—still the beautiful red-haired girl to him— fussed over my new dress and hid her tears behind the camera as she took a picture of me standing at the bus stop, about dance recitals, skinned knees, and my first home run. Stories about my first date, high school graduation. My first year of college. How happy and fulfilled they were to have such a child. Pages that prove how wonderful our lives once were. That was only seven years ago, but it feels like a lifetime.

That's when the old stories end. The year we lost her.

The year I lost them both.

The pages from the old stories are starting to turn ochre with age and brittle from the bitter truth that is his life now. On the new pages he writes about the horrors of cancer and the smell of the hospital. He no longer writes about faith. The new stories are about the lack of it. He writes about anger. He writes about guilt. He writes about death and the unfairness of it all.

He writes because he no longer speaks.

He cried so hard the day she died, something tore, ripped from his throat. They say it's not physically possible, but I watched as my father cried his heart out. I was there, and though more than one specialist says there is no physical reason—no explanation for his inability to speak—I know that the loss of his voice is as real as the loss of my mother.

He cannot escape the pain of losing her and I'm sure that if it weren't for me, he wouldn't be here. He would have died with my mother. His stories are proof of that ... and proof of the madness that's slowly taking him over. I don't know how much longer he can fight it. There is nothing I can do but read the stories that will be left behind. And I will read them all.

My father, he writes

Anna

*"I always thought they got married because
she was just too scared to tell him no."*

I'm sound asleep when my phone goes off, jolting me
from the fuzzy remnants of a dream. It takes me a minute to
realize that it's my sister on the other end of the line. With
the full moon shining in my window last night, I had
dreamt about her. Because the dream had been so vivid,
I'm not sure if I'm still sleeping as I hear her voice. I'm even
less certain when she asks me if I will come and get her.
She's never asked for help before.

"Becka? It's Anna. Can you come pick me up?" My
little sister's voice asked over the line.

I slap myself to make sure I'm awake, trip over the

covers as I get out of bed.

No questions asked, I tell Anna I will be at her house as quickly as I can and hang up before she has a chance to say anything else. I want to get there before something happens to change her mind.

I splash water on my face and brush my teeth in such a hurry that everything on the bathroom counter becomes soaked. Any other day I wouldn't be able to leave the place in such a mess, but not today. I admit I get a bit OCD with keeping things in order, but hell, we're all crazy in one way or another. Considering other traits that'd taken root in my family tree, I'd say being a neat freak is not a bad way to be.

I grab the same bra and pair of jeans I'd worn the day before and dress quickly, putting the t-shirt I'd slept in back on instead of taking time to find another one. I jot down a quick note for my husband, Ray, who's out of town. Leaving the note is foolish. He isn't supposed to return for a few more days, and I should be back home in two hours at the most. But there's a part of me that wants to let someone know where I went—in case I don't make it back. Even though we rarely talk about it, Ray and I both know my brother-in-law is certifiably crazy. Curtis scares the hell out of me.

It's been a long time since I've been to Anna's, since I

left the place where I grew up, and it's always a struggle to go back. There's nothing there but bad memories for all of us. Why Anna had wanted to stay was beyond me. Maybe she thought it's what she deserved.

When you grow up poor white trash, it's hard to believe you are anything else. I was lucky to have had Mrs. Williams as a teacher in the eleventh grade. She taught me that there's a whole other world out there and that I had as much right to be in it as anybody else. She cared about her students, all of us, but Anna didn't make it past tenth grade. After what happened to her, she couldn't face going to school. I probably couldn't have either.

Once you top the ridge, things change. You feel it deep down. It isn't the old houses or rusted-out trailers you pass, or the pathetic, mangy-looking dogs chained to the trees in their yards. It's not the tanning salons, selling melanoma and synthetic vitamin D with their cheap plastic neon signs. It's the air that changes. It smothers you.

Anna lives in our parents' old rental house. It wasn't much of a surprise when she said she would stay thereafter our parents passed. Hell, she'd paid the rent for the last few years they were alive anyway, and she didn't want to move. She said she didn't like change. But, how the hell would she know? She never changed anything. Anna still pays rent, still walks or rides her bike to work, and still wears her pretty red hair in a long, plain, ponytail down her back. Just like she has since she turned seventeen and took the job at Electrolux.

Only one red light in town and it always turns on me, like it's going to make me stop and look around. There's the old grocery store where everyone works at one time or another sacking groceries. And the gas station where they still pump your gas for you. If you don't mind the old fart staring at your boobs the entire time. Not me, I mind. I always make sure my tank is full at the gas station at the bottom of the ridge before making the trip to the top.

There's the drug store where we walked to after school on Thursdays if we'd saved enough spare change to treat ourselves to penny candy and a cold drink. It doesn't have a soda fountain anymore, but years ago I would get a vanilla Coke and Anna would get a cherry Coke at the counter inside. That's if we hadn't wasted our spare pennies on useless wishes in the abandoned well behind our house.

We used to call it our wishing well. Anna and I were certain it was magic since we didn't know anyone else who had one. It was hidden in a circle of trees and kudzu vines at the back of our property, back where the black-eyed susans and wild daisies fought the sting weed for space.

We found it by accident one morning—looking for a place to hide from the hangover induced fights we knew would take place once the adults woke up. You had to look hard to find it, but once you pushed your way through the small opening in the vines we made, the trees opened up to the blue sky overhead.

Anna and I used that space often. Under the light of a full moon, it did look like it held some kind of magical power. We would wait until midnight on the first night of each full moon—what we believed was the most powerful time for making wishes—and throw our pennies in.

Together, we would wish out loud under the light of the moon. We'd wish that our parents would quit drinking, that they would stop fighting—that life would be normal. Sometimes we wished for a puppy or kitten. Or for Gretchen Lynn, the meanest girl in school, to get headlice. For our uncle to run his motorcycle into a deep ditch full of rattlesnakes and hungry alligators. Going so far as to wish that if it didn't kill him, at least paralyze him from the waist down.

I would watch Anna, her face shining under the moon's glow, and wish that my little sister could forget what had happened to her that caused her night terrors. Those wishes were never spoken out loud, because what happened to Anna was never talked about. Ever. When she woke in the middle of the night screaming, our parents would act like they didn't hear a thing. I was the one who went to her to calm her down, dry her tears, and get her back to sleep. No one ever mentioned what caused the nightmares, not even Anna. But I knew.

Back then Anna and I thought our wishes would come true if we just believed hard enough. Until the day we saw our mama walking up to the well. She was carrying empty bottles in both hands, more pressed between her arms and chest. We knew what they were, we had seen the same bottles hidden all over the house. Daddy had them hidden in his truck, too. Bottles of vodka, whiskey, scotch, pure grain alcohol. Neither one of them was picky. We watched Mama stop and look around to see if anybody was watching her, which we thought was weird. No one could see her from the road or the neighboring houses out there at the well. The only people she could've been looking for was me and Anna, and we knew how much she drank. It was no secret. Maybe she thought she was better at hiding it, maybe she told herself that if there was no evidence, if she got rid of the bottles, no one would know.

After looking around one more time to make sure no one was watching, she threw all the bottles in at once.

Leaning over the low rock wall as if she were waiting to hear the sound of the bottles breaking on the rocks below. We knew she wouldn't hear anything; we'd never heard a sound after all the handfuls of pennies we'd thrown in. The well was a bottomless pit.

Pushing herself off the side of the well, Mama straightened her back and took a deep breath. For a split second she looked like the mama I once knew, the one who loved us.

But by the time we went in for dinner later that day, the woman I'd glimpsed was gone again—the drunken imposter back in charge. A glass of vodka disguised by an ounce of orange juice beside her empty plate at the table.

We never went out to the well after that. Seeing our mother use it as a way to get rid of her trash took the magic out of it. Our dreams of wishes and fairy tales lay shattered, as real as the shards of glass at the bottom of the well.

I try to quit thinking about the past and focus on my driving as I go by the high school. I'd loved it there. The clean, gleaming floors that smelled like wax and books everywhere you turned. It had been my only escape. A few more miles and I will be at the old house. My hands are sweating, and my stomach is twisting itself in knots. I wish I had some kind of protection, not that it would do me any good. Us Griffin girls are not known for our fighting skills. We've always been more like doormats. I'm lucky I have such a good husband. He's patient, kind, and understanding. He loves me and all of my weird quirks. Ray would never hurt me. Poor Anna. She doesn't even know what a real relationship is like.

Oh, how I cried when I heard they got married. I bawled for an hour straight. It hurt, like someone punched me in the stomach when she called to tell me the news. I always thought they got married because she was just too scared to tell him no. I came to visit her on her birthday, the last one she'd had as a single lady. When I showed up to celebrate her day with her, I was surprised to see that Curtis and a few of his friends were there drinking beer and watching football.

Anna and I went out to lunch instead of staying in and binge-watching the DVD's I'd brought like we'd planned. When we came back, Curtis's friends were carrying a big ugly leather couch into the living room. She'd laughed, trying to hide the nervousness in her voice and asked what they were doing. Curtis gave me a sly wink and slapped Anna on the butt.

"Sheeeeet, Baby Girl. I thought I'd move in, seeing as how there's more room here than at my brother's. Hell, I'm over here all the time anyway, right? And you know my brother and me get along like gasoline and matches. If I stay there much longer, I'm liable to kill him."

Then he told Anna to pick them up a couple of pizzas, tossing her the keys to his truck like he was doing her a big favor. And I'll be damned if I hadn't gone with her to get them. We were both dumbfounded, I guess. It was obvious to me that she didn't want him living there, but the way he took charge, you forgot you had a choice.

Happy birthday to Anna.

They were married at the courthouse one month later.

I knew Curtis was an obnoxious asshole, but I didn't know the half of it. Not long after they were married, Ray and I met them for dinner, and I started to figure it out. Anna had a black eye. She had tried to hide it with makeup, but it only made it more obvious. I couldn't stop staring at the black eyeliner, heavy mascara, and thick foundation on my little sister's face. She looked like a stranger.

Curtis finally asked me what I was staring at. Or actually, he asked Ray what his wife was staring at, but before either one of us could say anything Anna jumped in. She said she hit the side of her face on the door frame the night before. Curtis made jokes about how clumsy his wife was, Anna pretended to laugh, and I didn't ask questions. Just like we handled uncomfortable things in the past, we ignored what was right in front of us. The next time it was a swollen lip. I saved everyone the discomfort of lying and acted like I didn't see it.

Before I realized it, there were longer stretches where we didn't see each other. But we still stayed in contact over the phone, and Anna sounded good. I never asked, and she never said how things were between the two of them. We would invite them up for dinner, but there was always some reason why they couldn't make it, and we never got an invitation to come there. I continued to ignore the elephant in the room disguised as a muscle ridden redneck.

Until I was passing by her house a few months later and stopped by unannounced. I couldn't ignore it anymore.

Anna opened the door before I knocked and almost ran me over. I don't know which one of us was more surprised. She'd been on her way out to take the trash to the bin and dropped it when she saw me. I dropped my purse when I saw her. She looked like death warmed over. Both of Anna's eyes appeared to be full of blood. The blood vessels had ruptured so her eyes looked like two blood clots with black centers where her pupils were.

There was no way to disguise it. And no way I could ignore it.

I lost my shit.

Anna started out saying that it wasn't as bad as it looked. That it didn't hurt, and her eyesight was fine, like that was all that mattered. I told her we needed to go to the doctor, but she assured me she'd been, and everything was fine. I didn't believe her. When she said they looked better than they had when it first happened, actually tried to make a joke about it, I went nuts. She tried to change the subject, but finally broke down and told me the truth when I wouldn't shut up.

Curtis had been off on a bender and came home mad at one of his drinking buddies. He took it out on her. She said before she knew what was happening, Curtis threw her on the floor. He held her down, arms above her head, and cut off her air with his knee pressed against her throat.

She said she thought she was going to die. Once she started talking, she couldn't stop.

Anna said she must've passed out. When she came to, she was still lying on the living room floor and Curtis was gone. She'd been terrified that he might come back and start in on her again, so she called a girl she worked with. She came and got Anna and Anna planned on staying with her until she could figure out what to do. I asked her why she hadn't called me. She stumbled for a second and I knew she was trying to make up something, so I asked her again. She told me that Curtis hated me and Ray. That he was jealous and felt intimidated because we were close. She was afraid he would hurt me too.

She didn't want to get me involved until she knew what to do, but she never got a chance to figure it out. Anna only stayed with her friend for one night. Curtis found her and bawled and squalled and begged her forgiveness.

Then threatened to burn down her friend's house if she didn't come home.

He'd sworn to never hit her again, and she said since that night, he had changed. Besides, she said, if she tried to leave again, he would just find her and bring her back. And right now, things were good, really good. They were even talking about going to a counselor and Curtis had quit drinking. She sounded like she was trying to convince herself as much as she was trying to convince me. I threw my hands up and walked away. I hadn't been back since.

I felt I had let her down again, but I didn't know what to do. I'd learned over the years—with the help of a therapist—that I can't fix everyone else's problems. My therapist said Anna would get out of the situation when she was ready. I prayed that Anna would still be alive when she got to that point.

I mean, I get it. I've read all the self-help books and I've been to groups, but unless you have been treated like you are nothing but a waste of time your entire life, you have no idea how hard it is. Anna has had so much crap heaped on her since she was a kid. She doesn't have any reason to believe that her life can be better.

It's hard to explain, but it's easy for me to understand. I know because I could be the one there instead of Anna. For some reason I was the lucky one. I had escaped. Then a few months ago, Anna called me and told me that she was pregnant. I hadn't known what to say at first, but she sounded happy. I asked how things were, and after a slight pause, she assured me that things were better. Then she told me she had gotten a promotion at work; she was working in the office now instead of on the assembly line. I was very happy to hear that, and Anna sounded excited. I told her I was proud of her and that I loved her. I wanted to tell her I was sorry for everything, that I was sorry for not protecting her, sorry that I wasn't a better big sister. But I didn't know how. We said goodbye after a few minutes, and I cried for the rest of the day.

Then this morning I got the call asking for help and I can't get there fast enough.

Anna is standing on the porch waiting for me as I pull

into the driveway. She looks so small and fragile, like a twelve-year-old girl instead of an adult. I leave the car running and help her with her things. The sight of five plastic Piggly Wiggly grocery bags full of clothes breaks my heart. When I get her settled in my car, I realize I'm shaking all over.

"It's okay, Sissy, he's gone. You don't have to be scared."

She rubs her hands across her belly. I hadn't noticed her cantaloupe sized stomach. She'd looked so tiny standing on the porch.

"Oh my god! I almost forgot! You are pregnant!" I shout. I knew she was, of course I did, but to see the round shape that looks like something stuffed up under the front of her thin t-shirt makes it real.

I reach over and hug her. She hugs me back, and it's then I feel her flinch.

I pull back from her and notice a deep blue and purple bruise on her forearm, it's starting to turn yellow. That one has been there awhile. The new red, swollen place above her eye will be a nice bruise tomorrow. There's another fresh one on her jaw, I know it's new because there is a cut which hasn't completely scabbed over in the center. I see what looks like finger marks on her neck, some are new, and some are old by the way they are fading. The collar of her shirt has slipped down on her skinny shoulder and I see what appears to be a bite mark—not a hickey, but an honest to God bite mark on her collar bone. There are little half-moon scabs where Curtis's teeth broke through the skin. I can't imagine what the rest of her body must look like.

I start to cry, unable to hold it in any longer. Anna looks at me.

"It's okay, Becka, we're fine. I was scared when he kicked me in the stomach, but she's fine. It's okay, now. Feel her kickin'?" She puts my hand on her stomach and I do feel something move underneath her thin shirt.

"Her?"

"Yeah. I named her Hope."

Anna then lets out a shaky breath and starts to cry, "I was so afraid he killed her." I hold her trembling hands and listen, an odd feeling I'd heard all this before.

"I talked to the police once, you know. Whew, that had been a bad one. I thought they'd lock him up for sure, because now it's two people he's hurting, you know?" she looks at me and nods, making sure I hear, "But they said there wasn't nothing they could do 'til I got a restraining order. They wouldn't talk to him or nothing. They said to fill out the paperwork, have him get his brother to get his stuff. Hell, they all know Curtis, they knew he wouldn't just leave.

"I asked them how a piece of paper was supposed to stop him. Would it stop a bullet? Could a piece of paper stop his car from running us down? How? Do you know how embarrassed he would have been if he knew that I talked to them? How mad that would've made him?"

She shakes her head and wipes her eyes on the neck of her shirt. "He would have killed me for sure. He always said that if I went to the police, he'd kill me, or if I left him, he'd kill me. He even said once when he was talking out of his head, that if I killed myself, he'd find me in hell and kill me again."

She rolls her eyes and actually laughs. "You know, he was probably the dumbest son of a bitch I ever did know."

Incredibly, I laugh too. It helps for a second, but then I remember where we are.

"We need to get out of here before he comes back," I say as I reach for the gearshift to put the car in reverse, but Anna lays her hand on my arm.

"He's gone this time, Sissy," Anna says, giving my shaking arm a small squeeze before putting her hands back onto her belly.

"Oh, they'll probably find him at the Pig Pen drunk as a skunk," I scoff and try to keep my teeth from chattering. Robey County is a dry county, but you can get bootleg liquor at the Pen every day but Sunday. I guess they have some kind of standards. According to what Anna has said in the past, it's Curtis's favorite hangout. That's where he'd turn up when he'd go on a two or three-day bender.

Anna has quit crying. I'm looking at her, but she's staring at her hands. They're steady now, folded protectively over her unborn child.

"When they find that son of a bitch, he'll be sorry this time. We'll make sure he gets what he deserves. You're going to stay with me and Ray now. He can't do a thing to you if you're at our house, Ray will make sure of it."

Curtis could push my sister around, but now that we had her, she wasn't alone. I wasn't sure what Ray could do, but it made me feel better to say it.

"They ain't gonna find him, Sissy. I told you, he's gone for good this time."

"Oh, they'll find him, Anna. I'm sure. He'll be back raising hell as soon as possible."

She lifts her head and looks directly in my eyes. She says in a small voice, so small I can barely hear her...

"Not unless they go looking down the well."

I start to ask if she's serious, but there's no need. I know Anna's telling the truth. I haven't seen her so calm and sure of herself since we were little kids. Before our uncle moved in that summer years ago. She shifts and reaches into the pocket of her jeans, holds her hand out to me and I place my open palm underneath. She puts her free hand under mine and presses it between her hand and fist. Her hands are small but strong and her skin feels cool against mine.

"I've been thinking about the well for a while. I've kept every new penny I've come across to use on a wish, just like when we were kids, remember? Last night the moon was so big... but when Curtis found me hiding out there, I forgot to throw them in." Anna opened her fist and filled my palm with coins.

She lets go of my hand and wipes her palms on her jeans. "Becka, I'm tired of wishing my life away. My baby deserves more than that."

I turn my attention to my driving, throw the car in reverse, and back us the hell out of there, spinning gravel as I do. We'd never go back.

* * *

In a rush of emotion so strong that it makes my heart pound in my chest, the weird sensation of déjà vu hits as I remember my dream from the night before. In the dream, Anna and I were at the wishing well back behind the old house. We weren't little kids anymore, we were young women, standing hand in hand. We both threw in a handful of bright pennies—every one of them heads up—so shiny that they sent sparks shooting out in every direction as they fell into the darkness of the well. The light from the full moon reflected on the new copper, giving off some sort of energy. An energy so powerful that I felt it again, sitting in my car hours later holding the warm coins in my hand.

In the dream, we threw those pennies in that old well and something changed. A weight lifted.

Anna might not believe in wishes anymore, but I did. And I believed both of ours had finally come true.

Charlie

*"You weren't the only one with secrets, you know.
I've had a secret of my own, one I need to tell you."*

This car is so beautiful Charlie, it rides like a dream.
You would love it. It's jet black like a witch's cat and shiny
as glass. I think it's a new Lincoln Continental, but you
know me and cars—it could be a Ford Focus for all I
know. That's your thing, not mine. But I can tell you that
the seats are upholstered in nice, expensive leather.

As I slide my hand across the seat, I can't help but
smile thinking about how much you would love the way
it feels. Of course, it's weird sitting back here alone while
someone else is driving, but I guess that's part of the deal.
Our kids, now grown, have their own agendas and

families to keep them occupied. Not one of them asked if I'd like some company. But then again, I guess they're used to me being alone.

The smell of the dark grey upholstery reminds me of the leather briefcase the kids and I bought for you after your second promotion. Caroline carved her initials and the image of her pet turtle on the side with Tommy's pocketknife. Oh, how she loved that. Caroline, our little artist even at six.

Did you know I gave the briefcase to Caroline when I found it tucked away in the bottom of your closet? Probably not, since we never mentioned your new Italian leather satchel. The gift from one of your girlfriends that replaced our gift to you.

My mind has been full of memories like that these last couple of days. I guess that's normal, but how would I know?

Hard to believe we started out with nothing. Who would've thought that we could make it on my salary as a teller at the bank while you went back to school?

And look at our kids. They're all doing so well, Tommy made partner at the firm and Genevieve has opened her third store. Caroline is living in New York City of all places, and she has an opening at that fancy gallery in two months. They're so much like you, Charlie. They have your drive and your confidence.

Something I lacked until recently.

I lived in your shadow, pushed so far back our own kids forgot I was there. Even the grandchildren call me by different names. I wonder if they even notice that Gran and Gigi are the same person, or if they even care. I'm the woman who is married to GrandPops and lives in the big house. The person that gives them presents and visits when their parents' schedules allow it.

Charlie, we had every material thing we wanted. But...there's so much more to having a good life. The guilt I felt anytime I thought of having more. Those thoughts never amounted to more than wishful thinking. Raising teenagers didn't allow for any free time to waste on myself. Tommy's drug scare, Genevieve's obsession with her married teachers and little Caroline's struggles with depression.

It was hard work, raising three entitled rich kids. Something I couldn't relate to. I was always the bad guy because you were never around. I know they resented me then, I think they still do in some way. I was the scapegoat in many therapy sessions. But luckily, they all made it through and are healthy, successful adults. I hope they're happy, they seem to be. But you and I both know that doesn't mean anything, don't we?

Three children, the house, the vacation house—why weren't we happy? Why did I stay? I should've left years ago, but at the time I couldn't. I was too afraid. But afraid of what? A life of my own? Bringing shame on the family for having a life of my own? It's so ridiculous now when I think of it. Then there were grandkids to think about.

Want to know something funny Charlie? I don't blame you for the affairs. I never did—I always thought you would ask for a divorce. I wasn't the woman you wanted, obviously. I look back and wonder, why did I put up with everything? Why was I so afraid?

You weren't the only one with secrets you know. I've had a secret of my own, one I need to tell you.

I've been having an affair with your sister.

Yeah, the one you call a dyke and only speak to over the phone at tax season when it's time to prepare your taxes. You're right, she's brilliant when it comes to finding loopholes. No pun intended. But she did let me in on another secret. Bushels and bushels of tax-free money set up in an account in my name. Imagine my surprise? I'm still not sure how that works, but Miranda is filling me in. Again, Charlie, no pun intended.

You know the summer when I took the kids and the grandkids to the beach house when you went on your golf trip? You were supposed to come for the last two weeks but said something came up at work.

Well, I knew about Tara. Everyone did. I wasn't mad, actually the opposite. I was happy, because for that month I felt like a person. A real person and not a shadow. There was no GrandPops there, spilling bourbon on the rugs and telling outrageous stories. Handing out money for every little thing.

"Two dollars if you're a good boy and get GrandPops a beer. Whoops, here's five dollars, missy, if you clean up that mess before I get in trouble." No wonder they worshipped you, Charlie. You were just a big misbehaving kid; a living ATM with endless wads of bills in your pockets.

But that year at the beach without you was different. We played board games without competing and no one accused the other of cheating. We cooked meals together without stressing about the time and no one drank too much or argued about who was making more money or who was Dad's or GrandPops's favorite. Not one single slammed door. We enjoyed the sunrises every morning without tiptoeing around hangovers and hurtful words.

That was my favorite time at the beach house if I'm completely honest. Something happened. I felt human for the first time in years. I'd hoped the kids would remember how much fun we had, but I'm not sure they do. As a matter of fact, after recent events, I'm pretty sure they've all forgotten.

But that doesn't even matter. The crazy, beautiful thing is— I do. That summer was about me. No one else. I found myself.

Miranda came down the weekend the kids left. We were all supposed to leave on the same day, but my flight got rescheduled. I'd forgotten Miranda was coming but she talked me into extending my stay. We spent the rest of the time together and we've been seeing each other ever since.

Oh, the secrets Charlie. So many of them... Secrets in a marriage are never good. For example, if I'd known about your hidden supply of Viagra, I would've warned you about taking them with your heart condition. But that's all water under the bridge as they say.

So, when you had your affair with Tara, and then later with Karen, I couldn't blame you. I knew then I wasn't what you needed. Charlie, you weren't what I needed either.

But something kept me from leaving. I still can't figure it out. Guilt? Disgrace? Lack of self-esteem? Fear of what our kids would say? Fear of being alone? Some people might say I was brave for sticking it out. For staying for the kids. But that's bullshit. I was a doormat for years, and there's nothing brave about that.

I thought this would be so much harder than it is. For over half of my life, I honestly believed that my choices had been made and there weren't any others for me—that being your wife was who I was. I thought that seeing my finger without the gold band on it would be odd, feel wrong, but it doesn't.

I hadn't taken that ring off in over thirty years, but I slipped it off at the last minute and watched it fall with the handful of dirt and white calla lilies I dropped onto your casket. One second it was there, the next second it was gone. How long will it be before the sun erases the white mark around my finger and I don't even think about it at all? I know this day was supposed to be about you, but you weren't the only one buried today. But unlike you I'm still here—I've been reborn. And tomorrow is a new day full of endless possibilities.

Enough rambling Charlie, and enough wasted energy on past regrets. I just wanted to tell you thank you.

Thank you for setting me free.

Lares And Penates

"Her voice was unexpectedly deep and smooth, like she'd been smoking unfiltered cigarettes since she was a toddler."

She was hard to miss. The first thing I noticed was her hair, the locks shaved into a partial Mohawk. Let me clarify, the style is called a Mohawk—she did not have an illustration of the Iroquoian people shaved into her hair. And it wasn't actually a true Mohawk cut where a strip of hair runs from the hairline at the middle of the forehead to the back of the neck. Instead, hers looked like her stylist became exhausted after shearing one side of her cranium and called it quits. The chameleonic tresses that survived the secateurs—sometimes bright fuchsia, sometimes neon purple in color, depending on the angle—was too extensive to stand up and collapsed over her left ear. The second thing I observed was the impressive number of facial piercings. There were so many metal objects protruding from her face she looked like she'd fallen headfirst into a tackle box. She terrified me.

The first time I saw her, I was certain there would be to be a confrontation. I predicted the scene. She'd be lurid and disruptive. I envisioned her leaping onto the tables like a demon-possessed Tinkerbell, kicking volumes of books onto the floor with her heavy, thick-soled boots while cursing like a sailor with Tourette's. Executing a perfect backflip from the table to the floor to throw the tapestry covered chairs through the picture window in the children's section. I pictured the quiet boy sitting alone in the corner while his mother looks for a new erotic novel running out with his hands over his head. Screaming for his life and leaving his mother to fend for herself.

I sent the boy a telepathic message of validation and encouraged him to keep running until he turned eighteen. His mother is an uninspiring fraudster who would rather read imitation literature than take an interest in her offspring. Who, by the way, reads on a much higher level than his mother and has far better manners.

I dreaded the interaction with the tiny Atilla the

Hun so badly I hid behind the rows in the Religion section. I let my imagination take over while I panted like a dehydrated St. Bernard in the early throes of a heat stroke. I would have to ask her to exit the premises. She would spit her gum in my face, perhaps even strike me in the throat or worse—punt me in the groin with one of her boots. And then, after letting loose a barbaric yawp, she would call me a freak or a fag or some juvenile insult before finally departing, slamming the door on her way out. The thought of what would happen caused me to break out in hives.

While I worked up the courage to bell the cat, no problems occurred. From the peephole I'd masked between two volumes on Buddhism, I watched as the girl retrieved her notebook and a stack of reference books from her backpack. Keeping an eye out for a switchblade or pipe bomb while my breathing slowed back to its normal rhythm, I realized that she'd come to the library to study. And that's just what she did. She tended to her business, was discreet, and didn't kick a solitary object. She turned out to be much more than the deviant delinquent I'd created, and I was able to get back to work re-shelving books in peace.

I consider myself lucky to have a summer job at the library. The red brick building has always been my favorite place to hide, here amid the alien corn of backwoods

Tennessee. In case you're wondering, I don't live in the middle of a corn field. I'm referring to Keats's poem *Ode to a Nightingale*. Like Ruth, I am a stranger among strangers. I've consistently found comfort here, and I am grateful for the job. My boss, who happens to be my favorite librarian, calls me her Man Friday. This secretly pleases me as I've had a slight crush on her since I was six- years old even though she is easily thirty years older than me. It's nice to be thought of as her right-hand man, as an efficient and loyal employee. I can't imagine another job that suits me so well. I don't have to carry on boring conversations with people, which is ideal. Since you're supposed to be quiet in a library, no one really notices. It took a while for me to get used to the other librarians, or I guess I should say for them to get used to me. When they finally quit trying to get me wrapped up in their daily dramas, it got easier. And once they quit *touching* me (little pats on my arms and quick squeezes on my shoulders) we got along just fine. It's not that I hate people—it's just that I would prefer to not be around them.

I don't like people in my space, I don't like the pitch of most people's voices and, honestly, I don't like what most people have to say. So much useless babble that doesn't mean anything. For me, listening to most exchanges is like watching monotonous television commercials, without a remote with a mute button to silence them.

Trying to make small talk makes me anxious and it's extremely frustrating. It's even more frustrating because I am a true logophile. Words, allusions, the forgotten art of wordsmithing are my obsession. And the reason most everyone believes I am an imbecile. Which is quite hilarious, considering *they* are the ones who don't understand *me*. But I guess they are correct about me in the long run. I am completely ignorant when it comes to reading people. It's not what they say that I don't understand, it's humans in general.

For example, so many facial expressions are overly dramatic and condescending. Most people smile with their mouths—gargantuan grins that might activate wrinkles otherwise known as crow's feet above the cheekbone—but it never reaches their eyes. My mother is the queen of contradictory eyes. And then there's the exaggerated look of interest when someone asks you a question. As soon as you start to answer, their eyes glaze over and you know they're thinking about a shopping list or wondering if they turned off the coffee maker before leaving their house. They're still looking at you, possibly nodding and arching a brow, but they aren't seeing you. I'd much rather be surrounded by books and the steadfast rules of the Dewey decimal system.

But the girl with the unconventional hair turned out to be a pleasant surprise.

She came in every Tuesday and Thursday and followed the same ritual. Notebook and schoolbooks retrieved from her backpack and placed on the table to the left of the door. Any books she used at the library went back on the shelf in the correct spot. She never had a soda or loud crunchy snack. She was unobtrusive, intelligent, and didn't go around touching everybody.

One Thursday, I stepped outside to get some fresh air. I slipped out the side door and sat on the steps in my regular spot far from the madding crowd. Okay, the library "crowd" is tame, but still. I like a moment or two to myself during the day. My hideaway on the steps is a semi-secret employee exit on the far side of the building away from the parking lot and I'm the only one that uses it. From there you can watch people strolling up and down Main Street, but they can't see you. I liked to sit out there on my break and try to figure everybody out. I would pick out the Mr. Micawber types. The young girls with their Electra complexes looking for Sir Galahad in every old boss they work for. You can tell the ones who found their Prince Charming by the way they dress. The way they look down their new noses and over their recently acquired breast implants at the fresh batch of young secretaries having lunch on the square. It's a regular Peyton Place out there.

I hadn't noticed that the girl was perched on the steps to the right of where I sat for a good three or four minutes. Smoking a cigarette, she looked annoyed when our eyes met. She didn't look older than sixteen—so I assumed she was on the defense, expecting a sermon about the health hazard of secondhand smoke. Maybe a lecture about stealing or using false identification to purchase tobacco. But I didn't keep eye contact. I had no intention of sowing dragon's teeth. She finished her smoke and went back in without speaking.

The next time was different. I was taking my lunch break, viewing the victims of conspicuous consumption through the leaves of the ancient magnolia growing at the corner of the library, when the girl showed up. She sat a few feet away.

"Ciao." She said in a voice that sounded older than I expected. I nodded, averted my eyes, and we pleasantly ignored each other.

A week later, she was there first. Like Lewis Carroll's Cheshire cat, she seemed to appear and disappear. I never sensed her near the door, but there she was.

I nodded to her. She nodded back.

It went on like that for a while. Sitting there together—but not together— analyzing the groups of people and enjoying the quiet. Then one day she started talking.

"Most people are hydra-headed. You don't seem to be. You seem to be more...aware."

Hey, I thought to myself, that's something you don't hear every day. *Hydra-headed: having many heads. The Hydra was a monstrous serpentine Greek myth. He was killed by Hercules – when he chopped off his head, two more grew back.* I shrugged my shoulders, too surprised to speak even if I'd wanted to.

"Have you ever seen a doppelganger?" She lit a cancer stick with an electric blue lighter that had a picture of a dragon on it. Or maybe it was a Nano Tyrannus—the fourth smallest known tyrannosaurid otherwise known as the tiny tyrant. It was hard to tell, but she seemed more like the dragon type to me. She stood there staring at me, but I didn't respond.

I was repeating the word, doppelganger, in my head. It had a nice feel to it. Made me think of riding a roller-coaster at the county fair. The small one, not the deathtrap on wooden stilts.

She didn't seem to mind that I didn't answer and picked up where she left off. "Because I'm pretty sure that my parents' doppelgangers have moved into my house."

Doppelganger: a double or alter ego of a living person. Often represents the evil or unpleasant aspect of a person's nature. I could sympathize with her on that subject. It seemed like once I started pre-kindergarten, my household was replaced by the doppelgangers of both myself and my mother.

I liked listening to her. Her voice was unexpectedly deep and smooth—like she'd been smoking unfiltered cigarettes since she was a toddler, and she used interesting words.

I waited to see if she was going to say anything else, but she was finished speaking. When she put out her cigarette (she always pinched off the orange tip and carried her butt inside to throw away—something I appreciated), I stood up to go back in. This time, she surprised me and came through the door at my heels. Inside the library, we resumed our roles; two complete strangers who never spoke to each other.

I found myself looking forward to our time on the steps, wondering what she would come up with next. In my mind, we had great conversations. I would come back with some extraordinarily odd, untraditional remark and she would get it.

Not just *get it,* she would challenge me with more of the

same. But in real life, I did the same thing as usual, repeated the meaning for the words and phrases that seemed to flow out of her effortlessly, in my head. I was plagued with a debilitating case of echolalia—a neurotic, involuntary echoing of another's speech—but at least I kept any response to myself and didn't give her any reason to ridicule me.

Lorn never let me down. She used words like jeremiad—*Jeremiad: a prolonged lamentation or complaint,* and utopia—*Utopia: a place of ideal perfection especially in laws government and social conditions.* Wunderkind—*Wunderkind: a child prodigy,* or Pecksniffian—*Pecksniffian one who is unctuously hypocritical.*

On the day when she was talking about needing to clean out her room, I realized that I'd met someone that I could have an alliance with, maybe more than just an ear for her to talk into. Possibly, we could even be *friends.*

That conversation started the usual way, with a cigarette. She—her given name was Lorraine, but she preferred to be called Lorn—said that her room had turned into Fibber McGee's closet. Fibber *McGee's closet: a closet into which anything and everything has been jammed without order and out of which everything tumbles when the door is opened.* She said she had too many Lares and

Penates—*Lares and Penates: Roman Gods of the household.
A phrase used to refer to cherished personal belongings and
household effects.*

Lares and Penates. Whew—that brought back a painful
memory. My mind drifted as I remembered the time I used
the reference of Lares and Penates to my mother. I was
speaking of her porcelain figures that she obsessed over. She
spun towards me with a look of complete disgust smeared
across her face and called me a freak.

"Just once I would like to understand what the hell
you're talking about." She stepped closer to me, so close I
could smell the sickly-sweet scent of mouthwash she'd used
two hours earlier. "You try to sound like a damn Yankee,
using big words so people will think you're smart. Just like
your crazy Uncle. It doesn't work, you sound like an idiot. If
you used *normal* words, people wouldn't always be asking
me what's wrong with you."

She kept getting closer and I realized that my back was
against the wall. I felt trapped. My mother understood that I
hated people in my space. I closed my eyes as she got even
closer.

"If you would use *normal* words, you might actually
have some friends. If you used *normal* words, you might
actually get a date and Myrna would stop asking me if
you're a little fairy." She was so close at that point I could

feel her voice on my face. Wet and hot. As heavy and suffocating as a horsehair blanket.

"I could have a date with a *normal* girl who would pawn her offspring for a ceramic teddy bear in a tutu?"

The words slipped out of my mouth before I could stop them. I hadn't meant to say them out loud. I kept my eyes closed, but I recognized what was coming; I'd been punished for much less. I wasn't surprised when I felt her palm strike my cheek. Not once but twice. And I wasn't surprised at all at the slurs to my character that came next. I'd heard them all before, just not all at once while being pelted with a rolled up National Enquirer magazine—what my mother considered a reliable news source. Somehow that made the situation worse. I don't know, but if she'd used a New Yorker for example, it might not have been such an insult.

My mother's story changed to fit her mood, but the main part of the story never varied. I heard it all over again as she swung the article proclaiming new evidence that Hillary Clinton was an alien from Uranus until her arm grew tired. Per my mother, my father left her because of me.

I'd verified the falseness of her claims through a reputable source years before; an uncle that lived in the state of New Jersey. Uncle Jerry, an introvert like me, was my mother's only brother and the last of my living relatives. He sent me a letter on my tenth birthday which I keep in the original envelope. That letter changed my life. Until then, the only thing I knew of my mother's older sibling was that he sent money to help his sister pay our bills, and he was a beatnik lunatic living somewhere up north. The truth was that he was an author of literary fiction and poetry who loved words as much, or possibly more, than I do. Uncle Jerry also suffered from agoraphobia after the death of his wife and could not leave his apartment. We never met in person, but he was always happy to take my collect calls that started immediately after I received the first and only letter from him.

Uncle Jerry was the one who told me the facts. My mother didn't know who my father was. Wait, let me explain. She knew he was a traveling vacuum salesman, Electrolux to be exact. Top of the line. But he, James Deer, disappeared when I was just a hollow ball of cells attached to my mother's womb. No one, not even my mother, could predict I'd be such an oddity when my father left. So I refuse to take the blame for him leaving. And anyone, other than my mother, would have been suspicious of a traveling salesman with the moniker James Deer. A conclusion I came to around the age of thirteen, one that I shared with my uncle much to his delight.

Inappropriate or not, that shit's funny. Thankfully, my

Uncle Jerry shared my sense of humor. And his love of words. Without him, I might have believed the stories my mother told me.

Uncle Jerry died a little over a year ago. Peacefully in his sleep, we were told by his lawyer, alone in his apartment. His old Royal typewriter now belongs to me along with the brass urn that contains his ashes, and a trust fund that I'll be able to use to escape once I turn twenty-one. Exactly one thousand four hundred and eighty-three days from today, but who's counting. I stopped talking when he passed away. I communicate only enough to get by—not to carry on stupid, meaningless conversations. Just enough to survive. Most people have learned to leave me alone and I like it that way.

Until Lorn.

She spoke like I spoke. She spoke like I *thought*. No one used those words, those phrases. Of course not—it's not *normal*. Like repeating the meanings to myself isn't normal but it was comforting. Soothing. At least I wasn't a pyromaniac. I didn't bang my skull against the floor or refuse to eat anything unless it fell in a certain spot on the color wheel. I recognize I have issues, but at least mine are minimal. And harmless. What is *normal* anyway? And who gets to decide?

That was another thing I liked about Lorn. She'd

never once asked me what was wrong with me. And the best thing about Lorn—she had still never touched me. You wouldn't believe how many people feel the need to pat and stroke me like the family pet. But once, she looked at me in a way that felt like she was touching me. And surprisingly, it wasn't an unpleasant feeling. It was after one of our fifteen-minute talking/listening sessions. She'd come up with some outlandish, obscure words and phrases that tickled the shit out of me. I must have grinned, and Lorn smiled at me, holding my gaze for an entire sixty seconds at least. I could almost feel her probing around in my head. For a minute, it felt like she understood me.

She said, still smiling, "You're not one for words, are ya?"

If she only knew. Words are my life.

I didn't know her entire story. I understood she was having trouble with her parents, she referred to her father as a nabob—*Nabob: a person of great wealth or prominence*, and her mother as Mrs. O'Leary's Cow—*Mrs. O'Leary's Cow: an unwitting agent of disaster*, a woman with the face that launched a thousand ships—*Face that launched a thousand ships: an extremely beautiful woman for whom, presumably, men would be willing to fight and die for.* Her brother, she declared, was a lounge lizard—*Lounge Lizard:*

a ladies' man; fop; social parasite, and a palooka—*Palooka: an oaf or lout*. A true Peck's bad boy—*Peck's bad boy: one whose bad, mischievous, or tasteless behavior is a source of embarrassment or annoyance*. Like I said, I didn't know the details, but it was clear by the way she spoke, the words she used, and the countless holes in her nose, eyebrow, lips, and ears, that she was as fucked up as I was. And I admired her for it.

Our afternoons had become a routine. One I treasured and looked forward to. I had gotten extremely comfortable and didn't think that Lorn could do or say anything that surprised me. But I was wrong. It happened on the day she was telling me about an argument she'd had with her father.

Lorn was more upset than usual. She was waving her arms in a corybantic frenzy. I thought her eyes appeared to be wet, and I prepared to console her if she started crying.

Lorn crossed her arms in front of her chest and spun on her heels. "Even though I had the last word, it was a pyrrhic victory." *Pyrrhic victory: a hollow victory, won at excessive cost, a cost that outweighs or negates expected benefits*. I realized I should say something, anything to comfort her, but I was also thinking I needed tissues. I wasn't sure if I should go inside for a box of Kleenex or offer her my sleeve. If she started crying, I didn't know

what I would do. I'd never been in a .
before.

But thankfully, Lorn didn't cry. She kept
told me how she didn't think anyone ever listen
That she felt like a freak. It was hard to hear, because ı .
that feeling well.

"My mother wants me to cut my hair. Bleach it a
nice, fake blonde like hers. Funny, isn't it, that platinum
blonde is acceptable but any other simulated color—
other than chestnut hued auburn or dark brown—is
considered to be attention seeking juvenile antics? Oh,
and get this. She wants me to go to her old alma mater
and join her sorority. Puh-lease! I'd rather be left to die,
tied over a fire ant hill while country rap music courses
through headphones someone duct taped my head.

"I want to join the Peace Corps. I want to go to Africa
and do something that means something." Lorn shifted from
one foot to the other. "I want to make a difference. My
father isn't any help. He doesn't care what I do, as long as
it doesn't interrupt his tee time or make mommy cry."

She was really getting worked up and I was getting
worked up too. I knew I needed to do something. Even
Quasimodo—a deaf, human gargoyle—was able to show
compassion to Esmeralda. Of course, he was madly in love
with her. I wasn't in love with Lorn, but she was my friend.

My only friend. I would hide her in a cathedral and fight a mob if needed.

Lorn quit moving around and closed her eyes. Then she held her arms out beside her and said, "Let a hundred flowers bloom…"

To which I replied, in a voice she'd never heard before, "… and a hundred schools of thought contend. Mao Tse-Tung, 1957."

"He speaks!" she opened her eyes and beamed at me. Her smile was so real, so genuine that it caused me to smile back at her. It felt odd—in a decent sort of way.

"Hallelujah! *You can talk*! You aren't some mute troglodyte after all!" She stuck her tongue out to let me know she was teasing and laughed out loud.

I amazed myself by laughing with her. Then answered in a strong, clear voice that was as new to me as it was to her, "No, not a mute troglodyte. A mute inglorious Milton."

"Aha," Lorn pointed her slender index finger in my direction, "I knew it. A potential genius of promise unfulfilled through lack of opportunity."

She quoted the definition for my self-description word for word, but hearing it spoken in her voice the reference sounded boisterous.

I quickly added, "Actually, more like Walter Mitty.

Except that I have no imaginings of heroic adventures." Or a wife, of course not. I'm only seventeen—and had never had a girlfriend. No, it's my mother who's pecked away at my self-confidence.

"You are a riddle wrapped in a mystery inside an enigma." Lorn raised an eyebrow and smugly placed a Marlboro in the corner of her mouth.

"I would take that as a compliment, but since the term was originally used to describe Stalin in 1939..." I said without any effort at all.

Lorn's mouth fell open. Her cigarette hit the ground unnoticed.

"*You* are the riddle wrapped in a mystery." I was suddenly aware of how perfect Lorn's lips were, regardless of the two metal hoops attached in the corner. "With your rebellious outer layer and your euphonious voice and vocabulary."

It was my turn to point a finger which was less than an inch away from Lorn's nose because she'd stepped closer, crushing her unlit Marlboro under her heel in the process. I didn't have the urge to move away that I usually had when people got in my space. On the contrary, I wanted to see what it felt like if she took another step closer.

I realized I was talking without thinking. All the words I'd been saving up to tell Lorn were finding their way out.

"I'm a prisoner of my own making, trapped inside myself with an overcharged imagination, and an abundance of useless knowledge."

She did step closer and took my hand in hers. I felt a surge run up my arm to my shoulder, across my chest and up my neck, causing my heart to stutter and my face to flush. Not once had I ever felt anything so nice.

Lorn smiled at me with her whole face and I smiled back. "I never expected to meet someone my age, any age for that matter, who would understand me. Words have been my only friend until I met you. Humans are so disappointing."

Lorn stood on her tiptoes as she spoke and looked me in the eye. Then she quickly pressed her lips to my cheek before she stepped away.

"But you, my friend…you are…wonderful."

And for the first time in my life, I was at a loss for words.

Acknowledgements

I would've never found the courage or the validation to put the words on the page without a wonderful human being named Elkin Brown. He was my biggest supporter, best beer drinking buddy, and friend. Elkin was an English professor at Vol State University who pushed me—a high school dropout—to submit my very first story to a competition. I think he was more excited than I was when it won first place. The very first time I stepped into a college classroom was to read to his creative writing class. RIP, dear friend. When it's quiet I can hear you playing your guitar, so I know you're near and you know what's going on. Cheers!

DeeDee Ferruccio, Robert Stone, Robert Knowles, and Pam Hadjisavalos. My first writer's group gang! I love you guys more than you'll ever know. Thank you for introducing me to Elkin and for everything else. So many good memories!

Michael Turner, thank you and everyone involved with The Nashville Writer's Meetup group for including me in the fun.

A big thanks to Sonny Brewer, who I met years ago in

Atlanta at a writing conference he and Rick Bragg held called, "Don't Quit Your Day Job". Seven years and several stories later, you talked me into quitting my job and following my dream. I will be forever grateful for your friendship. Those four words - **you are worth it** - kept me going when I had no idea where I was headed.

Tracy Redfern, thank you for letting me and the pups stay at RockARosa Farms when my life was upside down so I could keep writing and stay sane. There's some powerful magic out there in Adams, Tennessee. Thanks for sharing it with me.

Pamela Lambiase. Thank you for always encouraging me and pushing me to live my dream. Those deck nights with tequila shots, listening to Lightning 100 while we solved the world's problems and survived our own, surrounded by your beautiful flowers, saved my life more times than I can count. I love you to the moon and back dear friend.

Lisa Lineberry. Thank you for always reminding me who I am.

Karen Newman. Thanks for the early edits, laughs, and encouragement. Even though the plans changed, we had fun. Good luck to you in your publishing endeavors.

Richard Bailey aka #3, as far as ex-husbands go, you're my favorite. Thanks for all the stories. You were a goldmine.

Special thanks to these three powerful, insanely talented, and incredibly nice women. Thank you, Suzanne Hudson, for your wicked sense of humor, amazing talent, and all of your encouragement. To River Jordan, for your magic, your unbelievable support, and love of the written word. I owe you big time. And to Susan Cushman, for your time and invaluable advice. I thankee kindly.

To my Tennessee family, I love you. Come visit.

A big thanks to everyone I worked with in pediatric cardiology at Monroe Carroll, Jr Children's Hospital. You all had to deal with a writer disguised as a cardiac sonographer, put up with my eccentricities without locking me in a closet, and were always willing to read the latest project. I know it wasn't easy.

And a big fat thank you to my Florida *framily*. I am so lucky to have found a new home where I feel like I'm surrounded by old friends. I couldn't have finished this collection while working on my house without y'all. Thank you, Laurel Strong, Kati, Nasarian, and Nooretet McClurg, and Thomas and Russell Daniels. From low country boils to Thanksgiving dinner in August, for keeping me sane with games of Farkle and Golden Girl's reruns to fall asleep to on your couch when I was too busy to sleep at home. For all the meals and home baked treats, surprise visits from the grass cutting fairy, and help rounding up my wild dogs when Curly figured out how to open the fence. Thank you for keeping me (and my dogs and turtle) fed and hydrated, and making me laugh until I hurt.

Last but not least, thank *you* for reading. Without you—dear, sweet, beautiful, readers—these stories would still be looking for a home.

Xo

I'm currently working on a second collection of short stories – Sharp as a Serpent's Tooth – Eva and other stories, and a novel titled With a New Tongue Spoken, so if you like what you've read here, there's more coming!

My website, www.mandyhaynes.com will keep you up to date on future projects, and events.

I have a neglected blog - www.therunawaywriter.com that will fill you in on how and when I got to Fernandina if you're curious.

You can also find me on Facebook or Instagram. Just look for pictures of the pups and the turtle and you've found the right place.

And remember, we cain't all be saints,
but we can all be kind.